"Do you want your child back?"

"Of course I do!"

"Smile then—and get out there with me. Let the reporters have a good look at my future wife. Hold your head high. Hold my hand."

Her palm felt cool when she slipped it inside his, small, and he gave it a clench as he guided her around the corner. She walked easily beside him, but a hint of alarm still lingered in her voice. "Landon, I feel like all these people can see right through me. That they know this is a farce and that I have no clue who you are."

"Do me a favor, Beth?"

"What?"

"Act like you love me."

Dear Reader,

We've all made mistakes in our lives. Some minor. Some big.

But what about when those mistakes shape us for the rest of our lives and take the one thing we love most from us?

What if you choose the wrong husband and years later he takes away your beloved son?

And what if the only hope of getting that innocent boy back is to ask for help from the one man whom you've always thought was an enemy?

These were the kind of questions that popped through my mind as I wrote Beth and Landon's story—a story I absolutely *love!*

I mean, just imagine having to ask your sworn enemy for a favor…how difficult asking for this favor would be, how embarrassed you'd feel, and how determined and desperate you'd have to be in order to go through with it.

Now, imagine *his* side: your enemy's ex-wife desperately attempting to bargain with you, and at the same time, stirring your long-dormant lust. Sounds complicated, right? And exciting!

Readers, meet Beth and Landon.

A woman who wants her son back.

A man who wants his life back.

Enemies joined by one common goal: revenge.

They're both people who think they only have vengeance in their hearts. What a lovely and thrilling surprise it would be, if they discovered they had something more…

I hope you enjoy their story!

Red

Paper Marriage Proposition

RED GARNIER

MILLS & BOON®

First published in Great Britain 2011
by Mills & Boon, an imprint of Harlequin (UK) Limited.
Large Print edition 2011
Harlequin (UK) Limited,
Eton House, 18-24 Paradise Road,
Richmond, Surrey TW9 1SR

© Red Garnier 2011

ISBN: 978 0 263 21781 1

Harlequin (UK) policy is to use papers that are natural,
renewable and recyclable products and made from
wood grown in sustainable forests. The logging
and manufacturing process conform to the legal
environmental regulations of the country of origin.

Printed and bound in Great Britain
by CPI Antony Rowe, Chippenham, Wiltshire

RED GARNIER

is a fan of books, chocolate and happily ever afters. What better way to spend the day than combining all three? Travelling frequently between the United States and Mexico, Red likes to call Texas home. She'd love to hear from her readers at redgarnier@gmail.com. For more on upcoming books and current contests, please visit her website, www.redgarnier.com

As always, with my deepest thanks
to—Krista, Charles and Shana.
Thank you for making this book shine.

This book is dedicated to
my flesh-and-blood hero.

One

Desperate.

Desperate was the only word to describe her at this point, the only word to justify what she was doing.

Her heart rattled in her chest, and her clammy hands shook so hard she could barely control them.

She was stepping into a man's hotel room—uninvited.

She had lied to the housekeeper to gain access, and this only after days of having groveled to this elusive stranger's secretary and attempting to bribe his chauffeur. And now, as she embarked on her first felony, Bethany Lewis expected to crack under the pressure.

Legs trembling, she shut the door behind her,

pulled out a little black book and clutched it to her chest as she eased deeper into the presidential suite—uninvited.

The space was lit by soft lamplight, scented with the sweet smell of oranges. Her stomach rumbled, still starved for today's breakfast, lunch and dinner.

A small lacquered desk sat by the window. Behind it, the satin, peach-colored drapes were gathered aside to reveal a wide balcony overlooking the city. A silver tray with chocolate-dipped strawberries, an assortment of cheeses and polished fresh fruit was laid out on a glass coffee table. Next to a single unopened envelope that read *Mr. Landon Gage.*

The name was synonymous with old money, sophistication, power. For years it had been whispered to Bethany in hate. *Landon Gage will pay for this. The Gages will rot in hell!*

But the Gages were swimming in money, and if this was hell, then Beth would take it any day against the purgatory she'd had to live through.

She navigated around the Queen Anne settee, thinking of her six-year-old's cherubic blond face as she'd last seen it, wary-eyed and fearful as she left for trial. *Mommy, you won't leave me? Promise?*

No, darling, Mommy will never leave you....

Hollowness spread in her breast at the memory. She would brave a fiery dragon. She would lie and cheat and steal if only to make those words real to her little boy.

"Mr. Gage?"

She peered beyond the slightly parted double doors that led into the bedroom. Downstairs, the children's cancer charity function was in full swing. Bethany had planned to blend in as a waitress and make her move, but the tycoon had not made an appearance yet, although it was worldwide knowledge that he was in the building. Among the waiting crowd, his name had been whispered in anticipation, and suddenly Beth couldn't stand the suspense.

On the large king bed, a glossy-leather briefcase lay open, surrounded by piles and piles of papers. A laptop hummed nearby.

"You've been following me."

Startled by the rich, deeply masculine voice, her eyes jerked to where a man exited the walk-in closet. He swiftly closed the buttons of his crisp white shirt and fixed her with a sharp, ice-cold gaze. Bethany backed into a wall. His presence was so staggering, her breath wheezed out of her.

He was taller than she'd anticipated, broad, dark and intimidating as a night demon. His body was fit and toned under the dress shirt and tailored black slacks, and the damp hair that was slicked behind his wide forehead revealed a face that was both utterly virile and sophisticated. His eyes—an old, tarnished silver color—were weary and remote, somehow empty-looking.

"I'm sorry," she said when she realized she was gaping.

He took in her physique. His gaze lingered on her hands, the nails shredded down to stubs. Beth resisted the urge to squirm and fought valiantly to stand there, dignified.

Carefully, he absorbed the knit St. John jacket and skirt she wore, loose around her waist and shoulders after she'd lost so much weight. It was one of the few quality suits she'd been able to hang on to after the divorce and one she'd chosen precisely for this occasion. But his gaze narrowed when he caught the shadows under her eyes.

Her tummy clenched. She could tell he wasn't as impressed with her as she with him.

He seized a shiny black bow from the nightstand and pinned her with a bleary look. "I could have you arrested."

Surprise skittered through her. He'd been aware of her? Hounding him for days? Hiding in corners, calling his office, begging his chauffeur, *stalking* him?

"W-why haven't you?"

Halting before a vanity table that looked ridiculously dainty next to him, he tied the bow around his collar with long, nimble fingers, meeting her gaze in the mirror. "Maybe you amuse me."

Bethany only partly listened to his words, for her mind suddenly whizzed with possibilities, and was coming to terms with the fact that Landon Gage was probably everything they said he was and more. The very bastard she needed. A bona fide, full-throttle, lean, mean son of a bitch. Yes, please, let it be.

Something had become clear to Beth. If she ever planned to be reunited with her son, she needed someone bigger, badder than her ex-husband. Someone without conscience and without fear. She needed a miracle—and when God wasn't listening, then a pact with the devil was in store.

He spun around, clearly put out by her silence. "Well, Miss…?"

"Lewis." She couldn't help it; felt a little intimidated by him, his height, the breadth of his shoulders, his palpable strength. "You don't know me," she began. "At least not personally. But you might be acquainted with my ex-husband."

"Who is?"

"Hector Halifax."

The reaction she had been expecting did not come. His expression revealed nothing, not the mildest interest, definitely not the anger she'd been striving for.

Bethany wiped one clammy hand on her jacket and eased away from the wall, still keeping a careful distance. "I hear you've been enemies for a time."

"I have many enemies. I do not sit around thinking of them all day. Now if you'll make this quick, I'm expected downstairs."

Quick.

She didn't even know where to begin. Her life was such a tangled, thorny mess, her emotions so beat up, her story so sorry she found there were few descriptors that would do it justice and no *quick* way to explain it.

When she at last spoke, the horrible words caused actual pain in her throat. "He took my son from me."

Gage slammed his laptop shut and began to shove the files into his briefcase. "Aha."

She focused on his hard profile and wondered if he'd known, suspected, that she would come to him. He seemed not in the least surprised by her visit. Then again, he looked like a man who'd seen it all.

"I need…I want him back. A six-year-old should be with his mother."

He locked his briefcase with an efficient click.

Tamping down an anger that had nothing to do

with him and everything to do with her ex-husband, Beth attempted to level her voice. "We battled for him in a custody hearing. Hector's lawyers provided photographs of me having an illicit affair. Several, actually. Of me…with different men."

This time, when his eyes ventured the length of her body, she experienced the alarming sensation of having him mentally strip off her clothes. "I read the papers, Miss Lewis. You've got quite a reputation now."

He reached for his wallet on the nightstand, slipped it into his back pocket and lifted a tailored black jacket from the back of a nearby chair.

"They paint me as a Jezebel. It's a lie, Mr. Gage," she said.

Gage unapologetically started across the suite and thrust his arms into the coat sleeves.

Beth briskly followed him out of the room and down the hall and to the elevator bank. Her heart tripped when he stopped. He slammed his finger into the down arrow, then leaned back on his heels and regarded her plainly. "And how is this my problem?"

"Look." Her voice shook, and her heart was about to pop. "I have no resources to fight him or his lawyers. He made sure I received nothing. At first I thought there would be a young lawyer hungry enough to put his name out there and take a case like this with no money, but there isn't. I paid twenty dollars to a service online just so I could see what my options were."

She paused for oxygen.

"Apparently, if my circumstances change, I could petition for a custody change. I have already quit my job. Hector accused me of leaving David all day with my mother while I worked, and my mother… well, she's a little deaf. But she *loves* David, she's a *great* grandmother," she quickly defended, "and I had to work, Mr. Gage. Hector left us without money."

"I see."

His steady regard caused a burning heat to crawl up her neck and cheeks.

No doubt in her mind that she was being judged all over again, and right now, it felt as humiliating as it had in court.

The elevator arrived with a ping, and she followed him inside, inhaling deeply for courage.

And to her dismay, all she could smell the moment the doors closed and they were enclosed in such a small space was him. Clean and musky, his scent unsettled her nerves. It felt as if she had pins in her veins.

God, the man was seriously, ludicrously sexy and he smelled really, really good.

Beth shouldn't have noticed this, but she was having trouble organizing her thoughts.

Landon Gage crossed his big, strong arms and gazed with notable impatience at the blinking LED numbers, as though they couldn't reach the ballroom floor soon enough.

"I do not care about the money, I want my child," Bethany whispered, her voice soft and pleading.

No one had recognized the good, loving deeds she'd done right as a mother. No one had cared that she'd told David stories every night. No one had paid attention to how she'd been to every doctor visit, had mended every little scrape, had dried every tear. No one in court had seen her as a mother, only a whore. That is all they had wanted to see, and what they'd wanted to believe. Bethany, and men. Men she didn't know, men she'd never even seen.

How easy it was for the wealthy and powerful to lie and for others to believe them. How much had it cost Hector to doctor that evidence? A pittance to him, she was sure, compared to what he took from her.

Lost in thought, she had not realized Landon had stopped gazing at the numbers and was, instead, scrutinizing her profile as she gnawed on her lower lip. "And I repeat. How is this my problem?"

She met his gaze head-on. "You are his enemy. He despises you. He means to destroy you."

He smiled a fast, hard smile, as though he knew a secret the rest of the world didn't. "I would like to see him try once more."

"I have…" She waved the book. "This little black book. Which you could use to bring him down."

"Little black book? Like we're in high school?"

Beth flipped the pages. "Phone numbers of the people he meets with, the kind of deals he's done and with whom, reporters he's dealing with, the women." She slapped it shut with some drama. "Everything is here—everything. And I will give this book to you if you help me."

He stared fiercely at the little black book, then into her face. "And Halifax hasn't noticed this book is…in his ex-wife's hands?"

"He thinks it fell overboard the day he took me yachting."

A dangerous fire sparked in Landon's eyes; a dark, forgotten vendetta coming to life.

But the elevator jerked to a halt, and his expression eased, once again calm and controlled. "Revenge is tiring, Miss Lewis. I'm not a man who makes a living at it."

And then he swept out past the doors, stalking into the noisy, swirling ballroom, and Bethany felt her heart implode like a soda can crushed under his foot.

Music and laughter boomed. Jewels glinted under the chandelier light. Beth could see the top of his silky ebony hair as he wound through the sea of elegantly dressed people and soaring marble columns. She could see him—her one and only chance— walking away from her. And all she could think of was *no.*

Waiters twirled around with armfuls of canapés, and Bethany methodically maneuvered around the crowd. She caught up with him by the sloshing wine fountain as he snatched up a glass.

"Mr. Gage," she began.

He didn't break stride as he tossed back the liquid. "Go home, Miss Lewis."

Beth sprinted three steps ahead of him and raised the black book with imploring hands. "Please listen to me."

He halted, set the empty glass on a passing tray, then stretched his hand out to her, palm up. "All right, let's see the goddamned book."

"No." The book went back to her chest, protected with both hands. "I'll let you see the book when you marry me," she explained.

"Pardon?"

"Please. I need my circumstances to change so I can get custody. Hector will hate the idea of you having me as a wife. He will…he will want me back. He will fear what I can tell you. And then I can bargain for my child. You can help me. And I will help you destroy him."

Something akin to disbelief lifted his brows. "You're a little thing to be full of such hate, aren't you?"

"Bethany. My name is Bethany. But you can call me Beth."

"Is that what he called you?"

Her hand fluttered in the air. "He called me *woman,* but I can't see how that matters."

The disgust on his face said it all, how romantic he thought the "pet name" to be. Bethany did not have time to explain, for he'd plunged back into the crowd. Everyone, it seemed, either came forward or waved at him. Event security spotted Landon from their posts, and their quick eyes landed immediately on Beth.

"Look, I warn you," she said, bumping her shoulder against a woman who said, "Hey!" and swiftly apologizing before sprinting back to his side. "Hector is obsessed. He believes you're out to get him and he wants to get you first. If you do not actively do something, he will tear you apart."

He stopped and frowned darkly. "I don't think you have the vaguest idea of who I am." As he bent forward, his narrowed gray eyes leveled ominously with hers, making her hackles raise. "I am ten times more powerful than Hector Halifax. He'd dance in a pink tutu if I said so."

"Prove it! Because all I can say is Hector is happier than he's ever been. He's not hurting at all."

"Landon! God, Landon, there you are."

He did not glance up at the speaker, but stared at Beth with eyes so tormented they provided a peek into the darkest pits of hell.

Her heart pounded a thousand times in only a couple of seconds.

And still he didn't speak.

"Let me make this clear, Miss Lewis." Whatever she'd seen in his eyes vanished as though a shutter had dropped. "I am not in the market for another man's leavings—nor am I in the market for a wife."

"It will only be temporary, please, my family is helpless against his, I cannot even see my son! I crawl around the streets waiting for a glimpse of him. You're the only man who hates my ex-husband as badly as I do. I *know* you hate him, I can see it in your eyes."

His lips thinned into a white, grim line.

"Landon, are you enjoying yourself? Can I bring you anything, darling?"

Not even the fluttery woman's voice, coming somewhere behind his broad shoulders, could tear those lethal silver eyes away from Beth's. He seized her chin and tipped her head back. "Perhaps I do hate him," he said silkily. "More than you will ever know."

"Landon," another voice said.

His thumb slid up from her chin to explore her trembling bottom lip. A jolt shot across her body. An avalanche of longing unlike anything she'd ever imagined crashed in her. She trembled, head to toe.

"Landon," yet another voice said, this one male.

He ground his teeth, grabbed her elbow and began dragging her through the tumult of people toward a back hall, into a little room. Slamming the door, he closeted them in shadows. Only a faint flicker of city lights was visible through a small window.

"Bethany." He seemed to struggle to grasp the last tatters of his patience. "You seem like a smart woman. I suggest you come up with another plan for yourself. I'm *not* interested."

"But you're still talking to me, aren't you?"

"In two seconds, I won't be."

She caught his arm, noting his eyes were getting a

little dark, a little wild. She couldn't help but think that if she pushed a bit…if she pushed just a bit more…

"Please," she implored, her voice praising. "The public loves you. The court will want to know my new husband to believe I am respectable. They will want to know how much you make and what you do…" Aware that she was squeezing his biceps— very hard, very strong biceps—and that he'd gone rigid as if he didn't want her to, she let go. "You're an enigma, Mr. Gage. You give to charities. You… you're adored by the media."

Adored because he had been on the deep end of a tragedy. Adored because he—powerful, handsome, rich—had been shattered once, like a human being.

"The media is twisted." He leaned back on his heels and scoffed. "It is also mine. Of course it loves me."

"They fear you, but they revere you."

He glanced out the window, his brow creasing in thought. "What do you know of Hector's dealings?"

"Names. People he's bought in the press. Future plans." At the thoughtful angle of his chin, she plunged on more boldly. "I will tell you everything. Everything I know—and I promise you I know enough."

He silently weighed her words, considering. Yes!

She could see that he was tempted, sorely tempted. Hope spread inside her like a winged shadow. *Help me, Landon Gage, for Christ's sake, help me.*

Because she saw in this stranger's eyes the same lost, caged fury he must see in hers. And sometimes a stranger is all you have in the world when your friends don't hang around to watch the bloodshed. When they'd picked corners and they had not picked yours.

Landon Gage would understand. Someone, at last, would reach out a hand to her. Please.

He gave a toss of his head, emphatically denying her. "Find someone else."

Stifling a rising bubble of hysteria, Beth slapped an arm across the door while fiercely clutching the book to her breastbone. "How can you do this?" she hissed through her teeth. "How can you let him get away with what he did to you? He destroyed your life. He still actively destroys it."

She could hear the furious scowl he wore in his words. "*Don't* pretend you know anything about my life."

"Oh, I know *all* about it, I even watched while he did it. He did it to me, too!"

"Listen to me very carefully, Beth." His voice dropped, low and husky but laced with the unyielding iron of his will as he bent over her, a looming shadow eating up her soul. "It has been six years. I have put the past behind me, where it belongs. I'm not consumed by rage anymore when for years all I thought of was murder. Do *not* provoke me, or I may just take it out on you."

"This is your chance, don't you see?" She was grasping at straws and she knew it. "I thought you would feel what I do. Don't you just *hate* him?"

He pried her arm aside and reached for the doorknob, but she blocked the exit, experiencing a horrible sensation of watching her last chance slipping through her fingers.

"It will be over within a year, when I have David back. Please, what does a woman need to do to convince you!"

The book crashed to the floor as Beth grabbed his jacket, rose up on tiptoe, and slammed her lips to his, giving the kiss everything she had. Her lips wildly tried coaxing his, and her eyes flew open when he twisted her around in a dizzying spin. With enough force to yank the breath out of her, he pinned her back against the wall. "Are you out of your mind?"

She shivered, felt dazed and disoriented. Her lips burned from that kiss, a kiss he had not returned, one that had devastated her nonetheless. God, his chest was steel, his hands were steel, his annoying will was steel steel steel. "What will it take to make you help me?" she asked brokenly, sagging against the wall.

"Why did you kiss me?" he demanded.

He skewered her in place with his hands and the weight of his long, impossibly hard body. Her eyes widened. Her breasts prickled. An unmistakable stiffness bit fiercely into her pelvis. Oh, *God.* Somehow, with that awkward and pitiful excuse for a kiss, he'd gotten aroused.

And Beth was so…so *shaky.* She hadn't felt this in years. Ever.

"I…"

Wet by her, his plush, gleaming lips were the most distracting thing she'd ever beheld.

His fingers tightened on her wrists and his rolling deep voice vibrated across his muscles. "I don't play games, Bethany. My sense of humor runs thin and if you raise a little red flag at me one more time, I *will* charge."

"Lan, there you are. You're up for the microphone."

He abruptly released her and Beth rubbed her sore wrists. A striking dark-headed man scrutinized them both from the doorway. Interest lit up his features and made his lips curve upward. "And who might the lady be?"

"Halifax's wife." With that disgusted statement, Landon stormed out of the room.

"I'm not his wife!" she shouted after him.

The newcomer shot her a look of incredulity, and Beth spread her trembling hands down the plackets of her jacket, futilely attempting to regroup. She snatched the book, which lay open, facedown on the floor.

"Garrett Gage," the man said with a wry smile.

She hesitated before seizing his outstretched hand. "B-Bethany. Lewis."

"Bethany, you need a drink." He handed over his glass and easily tucked her free arm into the crook of his. He patted her fondly, like they were new best friends about to share intimacies. "Talk to me, Beth. May I call you Beth?"

Two

Revenge.

Revenge on a blonde, blue-eyed, tempting little platter. Landon couldn't quite push her image aside. Elegant in her blue suit, dignified with her chin jutting out defiantly. Bethany Lewis.

With circles under her eyes.

He doubted she slept any more than he did. He cursed under his breath, telling himself he did not care whether she, too, fought demons at night.

He should have been inclined to doubt her claims. A man became suspicious after the wind was knocked out of him…*I'm leaving you for another man…*

But the story had flooded the papers. Bethany

Halifax, now Lewis, had endured a dirty divorce and an even uglier custody battle.

Which Landon shouldn't give a damn about.

On his fifth glass of red and after the ordeal at the microphone, he downed the liquid slowly, forcing himself to enjoy the taste as he rested his elbows on the stone balustrade and contemplated the hotel gardens. The night had grown quiet, so that through the sound of water lapping against the edge of the hotel pool, through the sound of lonely crickets in the distance and the faded sounds of traffic even farther away in the city, he could hear his own thoughts.

Hector Halifax's woman.

Kissing Landon's lips like her life depended on it. Kissing him not subtly, but hard and fast and desperately.

It irked him immeasurably, her desperation, and he wasn't certain why. Perhaps because he knew desperation. What shallow company it was, what a lousy counselor it became.

Perhaps because despite his resistance, he'd responded to her. Why *her?* She was not even the most beautiful thing he'd ever seen, and certainly not that sexy with that man-eating fury in her gaze. But when he'd felt her coaxing lips against his, he'd experienced the strangest, most exhilarating ecstasy. With her, trapped between him and the wall, the urge to rip off that tasteful jacket and fill his hands with her, fill her mouth with his tongue, had been more than he could bear.

He should've tasted her. He hadn't felt this bothered, this turned-on, in years. He should've tasted that mobile, hungry little mouth—was it sweet? Hot?

He tensed when behind him, long sure footsteps approached, followed by his brother's voice. Garrett. The youngest, Julian John, had to be around somewhere, too. Maybe necking with a waitress.

"I'm surprised you've stuck around this long," Garrett said, propping his elbows on the weathered stone.

Landon shrugged, not annoyed so much by the crowds when he was able to escape them. "I'm waiting for her to leave."

His brother chuckled, a sound much like Landon's had been before he'd forgotten how to do it. "I admit I'm very intrigued about the contents of that little black book."

Landon remained silent. He was intrigued, too. But he was the eldest, the cool head. His mother, his brothers, depended on him to make decisions with level-headed precision, not stemming from rage.

A breeze rustled across the nearby bushes.

"I don't remember seeing such hate in someone's

eyes before," Garrett said. After a charged pause, "Except maybe yours."

An old, familiar rage crawled inside Landon's stomach. He plucked a leaf from a prickly little bush, tore it in half, and tossed it aside. "If you have a point," he said flatly, "then make it."

"You know, Landon, I've been waiting for you to do something about what happened all those years ago. Mother's been waiting. Julian has been, too. You never mourned. You never got drunk. You went to work the next day, hell, you worked like a dog. You're *still* working like a dog."

"And this is the attitude you all wanted me to take? I pulled Dad's newspaper up from the ground, Garrett. I branched out online and tripled its earnings—you wanted me to get *drunk?*"

"No," he admitted, contrite. "I wanted you to do something that will balance things out. I think it's long past the time you took a hand to this. You know goddamned well you can crush him."

"Halifax?"

A glint of mischief sparked in Garrett's eyes. "Don't tell me you haven't thought about it."

"Every night."

"There you go." With a satisfied grunt, Garrett emptied his wineglass and set it aside. "Landon, come on. You're the loneliest bastard I know. We've stood by for six years watching you close yourself off. You're not even interested in women anymore. The anger is reeking off your pores, its eating you inside."

Landon rubbed two fingers up the length of his nose, his temples beginning to throb. "Back off, Garrett."

"Why not take your revenge, brother?"

He didn't know what happened. One moment he clutched his wine and the next the glass shattered on the nearest stone pillar, the shards scattering across the floor. "Because it will not bring them back!" he roared. "I can goddamned kill him and they're still. Not. Coming. Back!"

The silence that followed felt like a noose around his throat. He'd said too much, had lost control, showed his brother just how very close he was to losing it, how perilous he found each day to be. How pointless it all seemed. Power, respect, even life itself. It was all one big nothing.

Landon felt *nothing* but…hollow.

"Damn it," he muttered, cursing himself and that female for bringing thoughts of Hector Halifax to the forefront.

Landon hated thinking about it, hated remembering, the phone call late at night, all the evidence the detective had discovered. But at the same time, it haunted him. How could he have been so blind? So fooled? Chrystine had been having an affair with Halifax for several months; the detective confirmed she'd been texting and emailing and stealing out into the night to see him. Landon hadn't known of her betrayal until the day he'd buried her.

He'd felt cornered into the marriage, hadn't wanted her, but she'd been pregnant with his child and he'd done the "right" thing with every intention of making it work.

He'd failed. And he'd failed to protect that chubby little infant, who'd already learned to sit, and grin and say "Papa."

His son had died because of her.

And because of Halifax emailing in the middle of the night, demanding of Landon's wife that it was *now* or *never*. She either went to him *now* or they would *never* be together.

Chrystine had been taking medication, medication Halifax had prescribed, medication no nursing mother should have been taking and no sane person should be driving on. Halifax had known, and he'd still made the demands. Demands he knew Chrystine would follow when he'd threatened not to "prescribe" for her any longer, vowed not to see her anymore if she did not follow. The night had been stormy, dark and though Chrystine had anxiously thought *now,* she would go to him *now,* the crash had said *never.*

Neither she nor her son had taken another breath.

Landon never again felt his son's tiny, dimpled hand wrap around his finger. He'd never see him as a young boy or guide him through the painful process of becoming a man.

"I know they're gone." Concern etched in his features, Garrett reached out and firmly seized Landon's shoulder. "Maybe they're not coming back, brother, but I was hoping you would."

Bethany sat outside on a carved wooden bench next to the valet parking booth, staring at the black book on her lap. *You've brought the anger back to my brother,* Garrett Gage had said with a marveled smile. *I might even thank you.*

She was still puzzling over his words, mulling over her own situation.

Now what?

Spotting Landon Gage's burly chauffeur lounging by the hood of a black Lincoln Navigator across the street, a man who'd earned both her respect and her frustration when he had refused to be bribed or coerced into letting Bethany climb unsuspected into the back of Gage's car, she returned his knowing smile and sighed.

She'd stopped believing in fairy tales the instant she'd realized she had married a toad and no, they did not change into princes after a kiss after all. So why had she ever thought a stranger could help her? The enemy?

In his mind she was a Halifax. She'd always be a Halifax, and he must *hate* her for it.

But Gage had been damaged by Hector Halifax, and although he had gone on with his life, the death of his family had been irrevocable. Bethany could still do something, would fight as long as there was breath in her body.

She wouldn't live apart from her son.

She blinked when Landon strode out of the revolving doors, his square jaw clenched so tight she'd bet it hurt. He swept his gaze across the moonlit sidewalk and, when he spotted her, skewered her with a look. He halted only a foot away. "When?"

"When what?"

"When do you want to marry? Friday? Saturday?"

Bethany gaped at him, at this big self-possessed man with the wild gray eyes. She shook off her daze, and the words leapt off her tongue. "Friday. Tomorrow. *Now.*"

"Be in my office tomorrow. I'll have a prenup drawn." He tossed a black credit card into her lap. "I want you in an expensive dress. Buy it. Look virginal if you want to get your son back. And buy yourself a ring." When all she could do was gawk in disbelief, he pointed a finger in her direction and gave her a grim, warning look. "You get nothing, you understand? When we're through."

She rose to her feet, her nod jerky. "I want nothing but my child back. I'll find a job where I can work at home, I'll never lose him again."

His fingers curled around her bare wrist and guided her close enough for the granite strength of his body to threaten hers. He was so big Beth couldn't help but feel…tiny.

"Be sure this is what you want, Miss Lewis. By the time I'm finished with your husband there won't be anything left."

With that, he spun around, leaving her breathless with exhilaration, gratefulness, strange little flutters in her stomach.

"Mr. Gage!"

He swung back to face her, running a big tanned hand along his face. "Landon."

"Thank you, Landon."

His eyebrows drew together. "I'm not doing this for you."

"I know. Thank you, anyway."

He hesitated, then retraced his path back to her,

seizing her elbow and ducking his head. "Will there be something else on the menu, Beth?"

Her lips parted, closed, parted again. "What do you mean?"

God, his face was cruel, it was so handsome. His mouth, beautiful. His eyes, entrancing. His touch... my word, his touch.

His thumb brushed against the sleeve of her jacket, giving her flutters. "I'm asking if we'll be reaching some other kind of understanding, you and I."

She clung to his gaze, drowning, seeing no land in the distance. Nothing but the determined man before her.

"What kind of understanding," she asked in an odd, cragged whisper. "I don't think I understand."

But her nipples were hard as diamonds under her jacket, begging for...something. A touch; his touch.

His expression distinctly famished, he reached up and hypnotically traced her lips with his middle finger. "I wonder..." His voice was terse and textured, and he watched her with eyes that probed into the darkest, loneliest part of her. "If you'd like to kiss me again, slowly this time. And in bed."

Oh, God.

Oh, my God.

She could see by those enlarged pupils he was visualizing this!

He curled a finger under her chin. "Are you interested? Beth?"

A shudder rippled through her. The eyes. So fierce and lonely and bright.

A needle of an image stabbed into her mind, this virile beauty, hot and hard and pushing into her, and she...oh, God, she'd die.

She'd felt the powerful, restrained force in his body when she'd kissed him; all of it, it seemed, directed at keeping from kissing her back. How would it feel to have Landon Gage unleash all that suppressed strength into her? She'd crack. She'd detonate.

She'd say no. She had to.

No was a small, hard word, and small people learned to say it the hard way. Beth had learned six years ago that the hard little word *no* would have meant the difference between happiness and despair, freedom and entrapment.

Now it had to be, couldn't be anything other than *no*.

What if he insisted?

What if he didn't?

"I think we should really stick to the original plan."

But her quiet denial, although logical and truthful, planted a small, potent little ache inside her.

His nostrils flared. He stepped back with a curt nod, and Bethany realized that the brief, tight look that passed over his face was hunger. "Good to know."

Within seconds he issued explicit orders to his chauffeur, and then he stormed back into the building—leaving Bethany clutching the little black book with one hand, and Landon Gage's corporate credit card with the other.

Three

"I can now clearly see why you haven't had a woman in ages, Lan. Maybe Julian here could teach you a thing or two about subtlety."

Landon was hunched over the boardroom table the next morning with the newest copy of the *San Antonio Daily* spread out over the surface. Ignoring Garrett, he continued circling. He did this every day. He did it before they went to print. He did it afterward. Every single day.

"I don't want a woman." Landon flipped to the next section. His red pen streaked across the sports header. "Twenty-four mistakes, Garrett, and counting. I suggest you wipe that grin off your face."

"So you just want *her,* then? Because this prenup—" Garrett waved the papers in the air

"—is a bit out of the norm. Jules, if you may offer an opinion on our brother's state of mind—what do you think of the prenup? It boggles the mind that a woman would sign that thing."

In a characteristically lazy move, Julian snatched up the proffered document. He propped a shoulder against the wall and skimmed through the terms. He said, in his usual flat tones, "Twisted and somewhat distrustful. Good, Landon. Very you."

"Thank you, Jules. This is a joining of two enemies after all."

Garrett shook his head, then navigated to the chrome bar and refilled his coffee. "You're setting yourself up for a divorce from the start, brother."

Landon's pen unerringly circled. A date wrong. A period missing. "Yes, well, this time both she and I will know it's coming."

"You forget I was there last night, Lan, and in case you didn't notice, you had her pinned to *the wall*."

Landon froze. He scowled down at the page, pen in midair.

An image of Beth *pinned to the wall,* vulnerable with her lips wet, her chest heaving against his, made Landon's chest cramp. God, he hated weakness. He took advantage of it in others and loathed it in himself. He dropped the pen, raked a hand through his hair, and blew out a breath, glowering at his nosy brother. "You know what the scorpion told the turtle when it stung its ass dead?"

Garrett sipped his coffee. "Humor me."

"It's in my nature." Landon glared. "That's what it said."

"And in English?"

"In English, Garrett," Julian interjected, "his enemy's ex-partner is now going to be Landon's wife, and he doesn't trust her."

Garrett blinked, shocked. He set the coffee down with a thump. "You were the *turtle* in that story?"

"Here we go, Mr. Gage." His assistant, Donna, strode into the room with her arms full of old newspapers. Every piece written on Halifax, every page with Bethany on it. "Some of these date back several years."

Landon moved toward the pile Donna had just set atop the table and began spreading them out. "Unfortunately, we seem to have snitches," he told his brothers.

"Seriously?"

"Beth possibly knows their names—she hinted as much. I want to see who's been rallying for Halifax for some time." He opened the top sample, skimming for mentions of Beth. He could do this on his computer, he knew. But this was the one thing where Landon was ridiculously old-fashioned—he loved the smell, the feel and the substance of paper.

"Maybe it's in the little book?" Garrett quipped.

Landon cocked his brow at him. "And maybe Halifax is in fact an idiot? I'd have to be deranged to base my actions on the writings in a book."

"Why are you marrying her if not for the book?"

Landon was not going to tell them. He continued to skim. "Perhaps I just want a war buddy."

Garrett let out a bark of laughter. He slapped his back. "Brother, you want another kind of buddy."

Landon opted for silence.

"Whatever imbecile tracks his own dirt in a book deserves what's coming to him," Julian said in disgust.

"They deserve Landon."

His brothers laughed, and Landon shoved a sheaf of clippings at each of them. "Either get back to work or make yourselves scarce."

Garrett settled down on a chair and, eyeing him through the top of the open newspaper, said, "Mom wants to know all about her, you know."

"I'm sure she got a full report from you, Garrett. Julian," Landon said, knowing his younger brother's verbiage was almost exclusively reserved for the women, "you talked to your friend in family law?"

"He'll be here tomorrow. He's catching a red eye."

"Good. Garrett, you're sending out men to cover the engagement party this evening?"

"I got it."

Landon's attention honed in on a heading. *Halifax's Wife Caught In Illicit Affair*. A picture of Beth exiting the courtroom was followed by a long, detailed analysis of the court hearing. An awful possessiveness fisted him in its grip.

Grimly, he surveyed her picture. Something in her eyes was like a plea, an innocence.

She could be a liar, a trickster, a tease.

And, damn it, Landon still wanted her.

It was that complicated, and that simple.

Last night, as he lay in bed, remembering her, he'd sought reasons for the lust raging through him and had found none. Except that her wild, reckless kiss had promised breath to a dead man.

He was a man.

She was a woman.

He wanted her.

He'd have her.

If he had to pay her, if he had to wait, if he had to wrap Halifax by the feet and hang him upside down for Beth.

He'd have her.

All right, Beth, go get him.

Her heart pounded frantically as she at last made

it to the top floor of the *San Antonio Daily*. With a fortifying breath, Beth followed Landon's laser-eyed assistant—the one who'd denied her entrance to see him a number of times—to a formidable set of massive double doors.

An unfamiliar sensation assailed her as the practical woman flung the doors open and led her inside. Landon, in a sharp suit and a killer crimson tie, came around the boardroom table to greet her. Her stomach twisted and turned as he approached. What was this? Anticipation, excitement, dread?

Landon had been called many things she could remember, but the word *gentle* hadn't been among them.

"Beth," he said.

He stared directly at her as he strode over. Framed by spiky, dark lashes, his eyes gleamed as they raked her form. Suddenly, she couldn't breathe, he looked so sexy when he smiled at her.

"Hi, Landon," she said, shyly smiling back.

His two lawyers rose to greet her, and Beth shook their outstretched hands. She'd wanted to look respectable today; she'd worn her hair back in a tidy chignon, a dark clean business suit, and a light sheen of makeup.

She had never felt so self-conscious and wondered if he approved.

Dismissing his assistant, Landon hauled out a chair for Beth and huskily said, "Sit."

She sat.

She tugged her skirt down to her knees as the men settled around the table. One began distributing a thick file around. The prenup, she hoped. So they could get this circus started.

"All right, ma'am, if you'll kindly open the document in your hands. Mr. Gage has…"

Landon's sour-faced, white-haired lawyer trailed off in consternation when Beth flipped the document open to the last page and asked, "Do any of you have a pen?"

Two pens appeared in her immediate line of vision.

She took the blue one. Landon's chair squeaked as he leaned back; he watched her with the intensity of a diving hawk. His brow creased in displeasure when she set pen to paper.

"Read it, Beth," he said.

She glanced up at him. God, he was an extremely magnetic man. He even looked grander once one knew about his reputation, but that wasn't what made her a little awestruck. It was the air of suppressed energy about him, his relaxed posture only a guise, for she could sense the latent tension in him, his hard-bitten strength. She'd tasted it in his lips.

Those lips. Stubborn and closed like the man. She'd shivered all night pretending he'd but for a second, a millisecond, opened them and let her taste all that anger and strength he so tightly reined in.

Aware of the heat crawling up her cheeks, she lowered her face, loathing to think he'd notice she was fantasizing about him by day.

"I'm not after your money, Landon. I get nothing, you said that before. And I'm poor as a mouse. You can't possibly take anything from me that Hector hasn't yanked away already."

If he thought he could discourage her from her marriage plan, well, he didn't know how stubborn she could be.

Landon cocked his head, a panther pricked into curiosity. "Prenups are not only about money."

"Miss Lewis, if I may," White Hair rushed in, face grim over the fact that Landon didn't seem to be playing hardball enough to suit him. A formal clearing of his throat later, he folded a page. "On your wedding night you're expected to deliver a little black book with contents of a personal nature regarding Dr. Hector Halifax. And as your new lawfully wedded husband, Mr. Gage agrees to provide for you in all the ways a real husband would as long as you cease any and all association with your ex until your partnership with Mr. Gage is terminated.

Any infidelity on your part would result in both the termination of this agreement and your marriage." The lawyer lifted his head to speak to her directly. "I'm afraid these terms are not negotiable."

Beth was so insulted that Landon Gage would believe the worst of her just like everyone else had, she didn't move. Eyes narrowed, Landon surveyed her reaction.

He gazed across the table at her with such a proprietary, blatantly sexual expression, the ring she'd just bought in his name and placed on her finger began to scorch.

She held his gaze, her insides in turmoil. "I was faithful to Hector for as long as we were married. I'm not who they say I am."

It took him a moment to answer, and when he did, his voice could've melted the ground under her feet. "I don't really care if you were faithful to Halifax, but I care that any woman with my name attached to hers is faithful to *me*."

Faithful to Landon Gage…

Something effervescent slid through her veins, and an awful burn arrowed down her breasts to the warmed, aching place between her thighs. She felt branded, taken in a way that didn't demand their clothes to be off, as Landon's eyes sucked her into their depths and filled her body with a horrible ache.

"This is a mock marriage, but I still can't risk making any mistakes for my son. I'm not and won't be seeing anyone, period." Her eyes narrowed as another thought occurred to her. "What about you? Will you be making the same guarantees?"

"Contrary to general beliefs, I'm not a womanizer."

"But it takes just one woman to turn your life upside down," Beth countered.

"I'm looking at her now."

His succinct words and their unmistakable meaning flooded her with mortification, but they didn't seem to have the same effect on him. Landon was utterly still; unapologetic, patient, male.

Bewildered, she pulled her attention back to the contract and inhaled once or twice, she couldn't be sure. Her heart was still doing that flipping thing fish did when they were dying.

She kept hearing two words the lawyer had mentioned: intimately acquainted. "Our arrangement is strictly a…partnership. Right?" she said.

A tomb-like silence gripped the room.

His lack of response made her edgy. She stole a peek at Landon, and the intensity in his stare made her close her legs tight under the table. Hunger glimmered in the depths of his pupils, wanting, *desire.*

Deeper warmth flagged her cheeks, hot as flames. "What is it, exactly, that you're demanding of me?"

More silence. His face was as unreadable as a wall as he steepled his fingers before him. "All I demand, Beth, is your fidelity. If you want to sleep with someone—you'll sleep with me."

Oh, God, when Landon spoke that last, her skin went hot. He made it sound like a promise, a decree.

And though romance and sex were the last things on her mind right now, his ill-concealed interest stirred *her* interest and made her aware of how beautifully virile he was. His body had to be the most exquisite living sculpture she'd ever beheld. Landon filled the shoulders of his jacket, his broad, strong frame overpowering the chair. The air was so charged with his masculinity, Beth couldn't help but remember she was female.

They engaged in an unsettling staring contest. The silence was finally interrupted by the brown-haired lawyer with the glasses who jumped up to the podium, sounding a bit flustered. "Well, then. On a private addendum that is to remain under Mr. Gage's supervision, we state that after gaining custody of your child, the marriage will proceed for a short time, until the waters calm down," he argued, his tone softer than White Hair's. "And when the moment comes to part ways, Mr. Gage expects you to grant him a fast, discreet divorce in exchange for a small settlement, which you and your son can use to begin a new life."

She couldn't believe the discomfort of discussing this—her son, her economics, her future divorce—in a boardroom, and briefly she thought she'd rather her seat rear back and catapult her to the sky.

For some reason, her body pulsed with Landon's stares, with his nearness. Each quiver and tingle of awareness reminded her of every want and need and craving not appeased for years, for a lifetime.

Stopping the lawyer in midsentence, she glared at the dark, still man across the table, and firmly whispered, "I don't want your settlement. It's *you* I want, you're the only one who can hurt Hector."

He betrayed no reaction, except that, on the table, his fingers slowly curled into his palm.

"Now, in case any child results out of your union, Mr. Gage gets full custody," the lawyer said.

Shock swept through Beth. "There will not *be* a child."

Her reaction was so wild and instant, Landon threw his head back and gave a bark of laughter. The sound was such an unexpected rumble, striking such a discordant note with the rest of his composed self, it sent an uninvited jolt into her system. Outraged, she glowered. He really thought this funny?

To risk a child for a little bit of sex with the man!

"You'd take a child away from me?" Beth asked, disbelieving. "Is that any way to start a marriage? An association? A *war* team?"

His eyes danced in what seemed like mirth. "The way I see it, Beth, we start with honesty, which is more than I can say for my last marriage." He sobered almost instantly, and his shoulders lifted in a shrug. "I distrust everyone, please understand."

Her chest contracted. He could've reached inside her with those tanned, blunt hands and squeezed her heart.

Beth understood too well.

He'd lost one child, and he wouldn't lose another.

He'd been betrayed. Just like Beth had been betrayed.

And when you stopped believing in people, deep down there would always be a part of you that you would never give, that nobody could *ever* again reach.

Landon wouldn't trust Beth—but he would help her. And how, she marveled, had she enlisted such a man's aid? She knew a gift from the universe when she saw one.

And there he was, sitting across the table—beautiful and ruthless. God help her.

No, God help Hector Halifax when Landon Gage was through with him.

The thought invigorated her, exhilarated her. It could've been foreplay for the way her body responded to the idea of her new husband stomping all over Hector for all the times he'd stomped on Beth.

Relaxing in her seat, she confessed with a mischievous grin, "I'm still marrying you, Landon. Toss any more hoops you want me to jump through, but I'm still marrying you."

A flicker of admiration passed across his face. Then the awesome silver in his eyes turned molten, his jaw bunched tightly—and he appeared shockingly…eager. A strange gravity entered his voice. "How about you sign those papers now, Bethany?"

The white-haired lawyer nodded in the direction of the document. "Miss Lewis? If you please?"

Bethany.

No one ever called her that.

Trying to dismiss the fact that he'd made it sound so intimate, like Bethany were his pet name for her, Beth signed the dotted line with a flourish and pointed the end of the pen at Landon. "Mrs. Gage," she said, correcting the lawyer.

Landon's eyes flashed. For a slow heartbeat, Beth pictured him lunging across the table, hauling her to him, and feasting on the lips he'd rejected the night before.

"I'm a Gage now," she whispered.

"Not yet." Slow and sure, his lips formed the wickedest, most dangerous grin she'd ever seen. "Gentlemen, I'd like to be left alone with my fiancée."

Four

A tense silence descended as soon as the doors sealed shut with a soft *click*. Then Bethany spoke. "I think we should talk about our plan. I want Hector groveling, Landon. I want him penniless, honorless, childless and whimpering like a whipped dog."

Landon's eyebrows rose.

He gazed at her and struggled not to show the way her words affected him, stirred his deepest, darkest appetites.

He had lied to his brothers.

She was so damned cute like this, murderous and practical, she probably didn't even know it.

Yeah, Landon had lied.

He *did* want a woman, and she was in this very room with him.

Somber, he rose and started around the boardroom table. His heart pounded a slow, heavy rhythm. "He'll be humiliated," he said direly.

"Publicly, I hope."

He fisted his hands. "He'll be a babbling idiot by the time we're through with him."

Bethany clasped her hands together and grinned. "I love it!"

Some unnamable sensation exploded in his chest.

He'd never had this kind of foreplay. Promising to run over the enemy while already imagining plundering the spoils of war, in this case Bethany's nice pink mouth. But he'd thought of her awkward kiss all through a sleepless night, and in his mind he'd done what he'd wanted to from the start and had taken possession of that mouth, kissing her wildly, savagely, and he'd been mad with lust when he woke. What was it about her?

He gazed into her eyes, clear blue, specked with gold and glinting with mischief.

In the sunlit space, she appeared younger and less preoccupied than she had last night. Her hair, tied softly behind her, framed a delicate oval face, her pale slim neck adorned by a small gold necklace. Her skin was milky and smooth, but what Landon could not get over was her mouth, and the way he could still feel it on his.

Roughly he whispered, "Did you get a dress?"

"Yes."

"White and virginal?"

"Beige. And decent." From her small leather purse, she promptly took out his credit card and a folded receipt. "Thomas is my new best friend. He told me you'd like it."

His forehead furrowed. "My chauffeur saw it?"

"I wanted opinions. I don't know your taste."

"Neither does Thomas." He took his card back, and the receipt, and felt a prick of disappointment when he couldn't succeed in brushing her fingers more than a second.

"I bought a ring, too."

He took the slim fingers she held up within his and surveyed the modest band.

Her hand curled around his and electricity rushed up his arm. The touch flew to his head like a bomb, heating his chest, his groin.

He struggled to tame the lust coursing inside him and thumbed the rock as though it were precious and not a half carat grain of rice. He drawled with deceptive casualness, "This is from me?"

"Yes." She angled her head back and studied him while he pretended to study the small rock. He noticed loosened strands of wheat-blond hair making her look sweet and vulnerable. "I like simple things," she whispered.

"It's small…" Like she was. A small little package, full of possibilities, shining the light upon revenge.

She sighed dreamily, as though she were thinking of that, too.

All of a sudden, everything about Bethany seemed to have an erotic nature. Her silky voice. Or maybe the loose, businesslike clothes which just made a man want to know what was underneath. Or maybe it was the hunger in her eyes, her thirst for blood. Halifax's blood.

Damned if Landon didn't find that sexy.

His mouth went dry as he remembered their mouths, blending, hers moving, his tight and burning, too. Surely he was making it out to be more than what it had been.

She was too thin.

And she couldn't have been softer.

She kissed too hard.

And she couldn't have been hotter.

Who was he kidding? It had been exactly as he remembered, and it had promised breath to a dead man.

"I worried you'd change your mind today," she said, retrieving her hand.

There was something perverse about wanting to cover that smile with his lips.

He'd played honorably once. For his son. But Chrystine's treachery had left him with nothing. He didn't plan to end with nothing now, not ever again.

He regarded her steadily, crossing his arms. "Has a Gage ever given you his word before?" Halifax's woman, he thought. And now mine.

"No."

"Then what gave you reason to doubt it?"

She shrugged. "I've learned not to trust what people say."

Feeling himself smile, he signaled to his adjoining office. Trust was important to him. His brothers trusted him, his mother, his employees—and soon enough Bethany would trust him, he'd make sure of it. "We should get down to business."

"By all means." Swiftly on her feet, she clutched her purse and followed him into the wood-paneled office. "Revenge awaits."

They were smiling as they walked. Smiling, together. And suddenly the thought of living with her and not having her was intolerable, not an option.

This little Buffy the Husband Slayer was going to be his wife, and he was making her his woman. This little thing thirsty for revenge would get her deepest

desire from Landon, delivered on a silver platter—
Halifax on a tray with an apple in his mouth—and
Landon would take his own justice one step further.

Bethany, her son, Halifax's family…

Would be Landon's.

"I'm organizing a celebration tonight at La Cantera." He moved behind his desk and derived a
purely male satisfaction at the approval in her gaze.
"I'm fairly certain it would help your image to be
seen at a small, tasteful gathering to announce our
engagement. Wouldn't you?"

She took a seat across from his and thoughtfully
considered. "I agree," she then said, crossing her
legs. "Yes. And when would the wedding be?"

Beautiful slim legs. Damn, what were they talking
about? The wedding, right.

"Friday at city hall works for you?"

"Of course," she said, her teeth white behind her
smile.

Landon had to tear his eyes away from her, as he
punched the intercom button on his phone. "Donna,
are my brothers available? I'd like them to come in."

"I'll get them."

It was important for his fiancée to get better acquainted with his brothers before the press flocked
around them tonight. Thankfully, within minutes,

his efficient assistant led both men inside. They wore their best, politest smiles.

"Donna," Landon said as he started toward Beth. "Have the car ready in three minutes."

"Right away, sir."

He shot both men a "behave" look past Beth's shoulders and then grasped her arm to lead her forward. "Bethany, you met Garrett, didn't you?"

"Yes, he seemed very nice."

"He's not." Landon brought her over to Jules. "Julian John, Bethany Lewis."

"A pleasure," drawled Julian as they shook hands.

Landon bent his head to hers. "He's not nice, either, Bethany."

She grinned.

And when that white grin reached his eyes, Landon thought: *I'm good as dead, just like Halifax.*

This isn't going so bad, Beth thought, relieved as Landon led her through the halls of the executive floor of the *San Antonio Daily* toward the elevator bank. Not so bad at all.

True, they hadn't yet discussed their plan in detail, but it didn't matter. Beth knew a lot of things about Hector. Little rocks to toss in his path. Big boulders, rather.

She couldn't wait to watch him trip.

"They're my brothers but they drive me mad. It's a chemical thing," Landon said.

As people stared in their direction from their cubicles, Beth frowned. Did they know she was marrying their boss soon? Did they know it was a farce?

"Your clothes are in the car?" Landon asked then.

She spared him a quick nervous glance. Maybe they just thought it odd to see their boss smiling down at a woman. "Yes."

"Excellent." His cool nod, combined with that same lingering, totally unexpected curl of his lips, made her return his smile. "There's apparently much speculation about you around here, Bethany," he idly commented.

She nodded, already having surmised as much. But now something else troubled her mind. "Where are we going, Landon?"

The elevator doors rolled open, and he guided her inside. "My place."

"Your place," she repeated.

"My home. Where you'll be living with me."

They stepped off the elevator and crossed the marbled lobby, and Beth was struck with curiosity about what the next couple of months living with him would be like. "It's a good idea for you to start getting settled in before the wedding. This will make our relationship more plausible."

Beth could only nod at his logic.

They rode quietly in the back of the Navigator and, twenty minutes later, arrived at the entrance to a gated community. Then passing a sprawling emerald-green golf course and sweeping estates, the car halted at another gated entry.

Beyond the forged iron gates, a two-story, gothic-inspired, gray stone-brick house loomed in view. The lawns surrounding it were perfectly manicured, lush and green.

"Wow. This is it?"

"Yes," Landon said absently, then seemed to come around from whatever he'd been reading on his phone and met her questioning blue gaze. "You expected different?"

She shrugged. "An apartment, maybe."

"You forget." He opened his hand; a beautiful, long-fingered, tanned hand that for some reason made her skin pebble. "I used to have a family."

A family, yes.

He'd had a family he could not recover no matter what he did.

Her chest gained a thousand pounds at the sad thought. No matter how hopeless her situation had seemed lately, Bethany couldn't begin to imagine the pain of losing a loved one so abruptly.

"I'm sorry," she said quietly.

She followed him from the car and up the steps to the arched entrance.

They'd died in an accident—his wife and child. One rainy night.

One rainy night when Hector Halifax had been leaving Bethany with her newborn in her arms to meet with Landon's wife.

Eyeing his stoic, sculpture-like appearance through the corner of her eye, Beth wondered what else Landon knew. What he didn't know.

As they entered the spacious limestone-floored house, Beth noticed two huge mastiffs near the darkened fireplace. They rose up on their wide black paws when spotting Landon, tails starting to wag as they padded over.

"Mask and Brindle," Landon crisply said. She supposed the fawn-colored, two-hundred-pound beast with the black face was Mask, and the striped, black-and-brown, two-hundred-pound beast was Brindle.

She took a step back as they approached to sniff her, swallowing back a gasp when she bumped into Landon's solid chest behind her.

Dogs!

And she thought this would be easy?

Landon steadied her, his hands on her upper arms, his voice in her ear. "They don't bite."

A shiver that had nothing to do with fear skittered up her spine. "Oh."

"Sit."

The dogs sat. Their tongues were a mile long and dangled lazily while they waited to do more of Landon's bidding.

"See?"

He still had not let go of her. She angled her head just a fraction, and their noses almost bumped. "A dog bit me when I was little," she confessed, for some reason thinking it appropriate to whisper. As though she were in a church or a library. "I've had a healthy respect for them ever since."

"Yet you still married one?" He smiled.

"I married a snake—it's an entirely different species."

When he continued to smile that almost-there smile, she could almost feel it against her lips. At this close distance, Beth spotted the darker silver rim around his irises spreading like smoke across his eyes. Her knees went weak. He really was gorgeous.

Was he seducing her? God, it was working. His touch, his voice, the heat in his eyes.

"These two are a bit heavy to roll over," he said quietly, clenching her shoulders a bit, "but you can ask them to shake your hand if you'd like."

"Later," she said, blushing because she began to see a little complication. This man had an effect on her. A huge effect. He didn't even have to kiss her for that. His presence was an open, blatant call to all things feminine inside her which she shouldn't, for the love of God, embrace right now.

"Good doggies," she said, staying clear of the intimidating pair while at the same time putting distance between her and Landon.

After commanding, "Release"—a word which sent the dogs plopping back down before the fireplace—he led her up the sweeping limestone staircase.

The bedroom they entered at the far end of the hall was spacious, sparsely furnished, decorated in a black-and-white palette that went heavy on the black and sparse on the white. A guest room, she supposed.

But a string of unexpected words popped into her head.

"If you want to sleep with someone, you'll sleep with me."

Her stomach twisted as though she'd just taken a plunge on a roller coaster, and she had trouble shaking off the thought of sharing that very big bed with the very big man standing to her right.

There was no denying there had been some serious vibes going on between the two of them back in the conference room. But Beth had to concentrate on what was important: getting David back.

Her life was a mess and she'd taken fretting to a whole new art form. She didn't need more worries.

Hopefully, Landon wasn't getting any bed-sharing ideas.

She peered up at his hard profile. Of course he wasn't. Landon was in it for the little black book, and for what she could tell him about Hector.

He'd entered the room first and pulled off his jacket as she followed. "This is your room." His jacket fell with a thud atop a corner chair. "Unless you want to sleep in mine."

She wasn't sure if he was kidding or not and didn't have time to decide. "I'll keep this one, thank you."

His white cotton shirt pulled attractively across his shoulders as he calmly held out his hand. "The book? Do you mind if I have a look now?"

"Yes, I do mind, actually."

He wiggled his fingers. "Come on. Give it over, Bethany."

She frowned. "I said you could read it when you married me, didn't I?"

His eyes sparkled in amusement. "We're more than halfway there—the sooner I see what that bastard's after the sooner I can skin his ass on a platter."

The thought of Hector laid out like a dead pig on a tray was too lovely to deny. It brought butterflies to her stomach. "All right, but only the first two pages. You can read the rest after the wedding."

She waited for Thomas to bring up her suitcase, then extracted the black book from the outside zippered compartment. "Okay, so let's talk about our plan. I want Hector to be left with nothing. Absolutely nothing."

Landon's lips twitched, and when she noticed she felt herself respond. Damn, how did he do that? Every time he smiled she found herself smiling back like a dope.

After handing over the black leather book, she followed Landon's stealthy movements as he hauled a chair out from behind a desk and sat. He calmly paged through it.

"So why did you marry him?" he asked.

"I was young and pregnant." Beth plopped down on the edge of the bed, suddenly uncomfortable in her skirt and jacket. "And all right, yes, stupid."

He flipped to the second page and didn't raise his head, his hard, aquiline profile unreadable.

"I used to wonder why he'd want to marry me," she admitted with a shrug. "I felt so flattered. He would call every day and ask to see me. Then I guess he saw what a good daughter I was to my parents. He wanted an obedient, biddable wife—like all men desperate to feel powerful want someone meek."

Landon looked up, and when his lips smiled and did that eat-your-heart-out thing *again,* she felt a strange elated sensation.

"You were biddable, Beth? What happened?"

She burst out laughing. "Oh, stop it."

"Did you ever let him medicate you, Beth?"

She frowned at the question, at the hard edge in the word "medicate". There had been times when Hector had diagnosed her "problems"; she needed to grow up, and get serious, and act like his wife. Apparently, he hadn't had any pills for Beth's ailments. "Hector specializes in chronic pain—and nothing of mine ever ached except my pride."

And now she'd grown up, hadn't she? Now she'd put all her efforts into acting like someone's wife— *Landon's.*

His finger slid down a page, and he read a name out loud. "Joseph Kennar. He's one of our reporters."

"He's bought."

Landon appeared anything but surprised. "Everyone's for sale unfortunately." He continued reading, his eyes sharp as the point of a knife on the page. "Macy Jennings. Another one of our reporters."

"Also bought." Then she added, with a bit of disgust at herself because she could not, for the life of her, explain why she told him all this. "Hector would do anything to ensure he had the best reputation. He wanted to treat anyone that was rich and powerful, and keeping his name clean in the media guaranteed this. But I suspect Hector did more with Macy than just exchange money and favors."

"And you let him?"

She let him? Had she? Just so he left her alone? "Well I…I guess I ignored him. I thought that… for David I would tolerate it." God. Stupid stupid stupid. What would Landon think of her?

"But then?"

He seemed so inordinately interested in her that she was grateful his head was still bent over the book. Otherwise, his questions and his unyielding attention would be too much. Still, she felt so stupid over what she'd tolerated.

"But then I couldn't do it even for my baby," she admitted. There. All right, that wasn't bad, that she had finally found her courage and left the sleaze. She'd sold David on the "new adventure" he and Mommy would take, and he'd been excited.

She seized the nearby pillow and clutched it to her chest, suddenly needing to hold on to something. Every time she thought of David her stomach lurched as if she'd been poisoned.

"I left Hector a year ago and took David with me, and I found a job at a flower shop. Hector made contact weeks later. He apologized, said he wanted me back, but all I wanted was to be free. Of him. I filed for divorce and when he found out, he ranted and threatened, said I wouldn't see a dime. He was right, I didn't. But I was still happy. Just me and David and Mom. But then he filed for custody."

"He struck where it most hurt," Landon said, slapping the book shut with a deafening sound.

He'd read only two pages. As she'd asked him to. And something about that, the respect for her wishes in that action, made the walls inside her crack a fraction.

Wow. An honorable man. Who'd have known she'd ever see one of those?

"He *did* strike where it most hurt." Beth closed her eyes briefly as the pain sliced her anew. "He tore me apart. I couldn't even explain or say goodbye to my own son."

And what is my baby doing now? Who hugs him instead of me? And when will I be able to hold him again?

"Hector will be furious when he learns we've married," she admitted, struggling not to shiver.

Landon leaned back in his chair and canted his head, his lips thinning in distaste. "Let the man stew for a bit, Beth. Wonder what we're concocting."

But suddenly it struck her that more than angry, Hector would probably be annoyed. He treated patients with chronic pain and he'd always felt above them—like *he* would never feel the kind of pain his patients did. But Beth knew that he did. His wounds were internal; and they had festered.

His entire adult life, he'd seemed irked by the knowledge that there was someone better in this city, someone he couldn't touch.

Someone the "love of his life" had chosen over him.

Hector had never recovered from that blow.

"I've never seen someone hate as powerfully as he hates you," she admitted, and a wave of embarrassment washed over her.

She should've done something before. Sooner. She should've run with her son the moment he was born.

Hector had married Beth, and for a time she'd believed he cared. But in mere months she'd realized the truth. She'd been the means to make another woman jealous. Hector had been crazy about Landon's wife, feverishly wanting what he couldn't have and loathing the man who had ruined his chances with her. Chrystine would've married him if Landon hadn't been the better man. And Beth had never seen a man so hell-bent on ruining someone for being honest, richer, better, like Hector had.

"He was in love with my wife," Landon said non-committally as he crossed his arms, a neutral expression on his face.

"I'd say more like obsessed. He didn't seduce her out of love, Landon. He seduced her to humiliate you."

"You're right, Beth."

The words, steely and loaded with the promise of vengeance, whirled like a storm inside the room.

Beth felt it inside her, like one would feel a death wish, fury, hunger.

She had never understood this hatred of Hector's—until now that it ate at her, demanded some sort of retribution, that she take a hand at justice once and for all.

Hector had lied about her. He'd taken *David!*

He'd turned her into a sick person who only thought of revenge. She'd never been this vicious but the thought of hurting her ex-husband held so much appeal she felt flutters of evil, cruel excitement at the mere prospect. At night, her fantasies weren't girlish or even romantic anymore. At night, she felt so angry, so frustrated, she imagined how good she'd feel once she'd clawed the bastard's eyes out.

Did Landon feel this, too?

Would he stop at nothing, like her, until they'd ended up the winners?

Her pulse hitched when he pushed his chair back and rose with the ease of a wild cat. A large, stealthy wild cat who'd insisted that if she wanted to sleep with someone, she'd sleep with *him*.

"You're certain you're up for tonight?" he asked. "The press can be exhausting and so can my mother."

She wrinkled her nose. It was a miracle a powerful creature like Landon had even had a mother. That he'd been vulnerable once. And oh, yes, she'd been born for tonight, she was more than ready for it. "Believe me, so can mine be."

His brows flew up in genuine interest. "What did you tell yours?"

"That I finally found a white knight." When he didn't smile at her stupid joke, Beth sobered up and hugged the pillow tighter. "I told her I was marrying a man who would help me get David back. She was ecstatic. And you? Your mother?"

"I mentioned she should prepare to welcome my new wife. She was stunned speechless after my announcement, which is unusual for my mother."

"But she knows this is temporary?"

He didn't seem in the least bit concerned, and gave a nonchalant lift of his shoulders. "I didn't go into details, but she'll know where I'm coming from when she realizes who you are."

"Were," she corrected, watching him head for the door. "I'm reinventing myself now."

His interest clearly piqued, he turned around and crossed his arms over his broad chest, stretching the material of his shirt. "Who do you want to be now?"

"Me. Bethany. Whoever I was before Hector Halifax put his filthy hands on me."

For the first time in many many years, she felt hopeful, and as she drank in the brooding dark image of Landon, she wondered if he even realized this gift he gave her without meaning to.

She could smell him in the room, cologne and soap, and the scent was oddly reassuring. A surge of warmth, divine and wicked, began to pump in her bloodstream. His neck was tanned and thick, and his hands were wide, large, the fingers long and blunt. She had always been fascinated by men's hands, and his were so very virile.

"Have I said thank you?" she asked, her voice strangely thick.

He was silent for a moment, then, his voice equally terse, "Wait until you get your kid back."

Her temperature spiked. He was frightening, so powerful, so male, that Bethany had to remind herself he was on her side.

"Landon," she said before he could exit, "would you mind if I invited David to the celebration tonight? I'd like to invite my son."

"I don't mind."

"But what if he comes with him?"

"Halifax?" Landon leaned negligently against the door frame as he contemplated, unruffled like only powerful, self-possessed men could be. "He wouldn't dare."

"But if he does? You will be civil, won't you? I wouldn't want David to be exposed to any violence."

With an amused, wolfish quirk of his lips, he shook his dark head. "Beth, I'm posting a dozen reporters around the premises so they can capture me ogling over you. Believe me, I'm not announcing to the world what we'll be doing." Did he just wink at her? "Don't fret. They'll think we make love, not war."

Five

Make love.

Was there even room for making love when you were at war?

The nervousness welling inside her made her breathless as they drove to the engagement party.

Landon sat behind the wheel of his sporty blue-and-tan Maserati, tearing through the highway while Beth replayed the phone call she'd just made in her head.

She hadn't expected David to answer; he was too young and was observed too closely for that. But to the nanny who'd picked up in his stead, Beth had explained about her engagement party and how much she'd love for David to be there. Beth prayed that the kindnesses she had shown this young woman in the past would be repaid now.

Say you're taking him out, she'd thought as she'd given her the hotel address, *take him out for a walk, and let me see my son tonight.*

She considered the possibility of Anna mentioning her call to Hector and shuddered. No. The next time she hoped to see her ex-husband was in court.

Facing her *and* Landon.

Landon studied her in the dark interior of the car. She shuddered again, this time, in pure feminine awareness. She'd never known she could respond to a man like this.

He wasn't even doing anything, for the most part kept his eyes on the highway, but she was somehow inhumanly aware of his presence and his occasional straying gaze—her own gaze felt magnetized to it. His darkened eyes said more than they should as he quietly watched her.

In his eyes, she saw vengeance, justice and something just as dark, just as dangerous she dare not put a name to.

"Relax, Beth," he said, his voice, although mild, powerful and commanding as it cut through the silence. "Trust me a little. By the time he loses his pride, his word, his company and his child, Hector Halifax will have no idea what hit him."

But it was Beth who felt struck an hour later, while their petite celebration was underway in the sprawling gardens of the prestigious La Cantera Golf Resort. And Beth knew exactly what hit her.

The sight of the looming figure blocking her entry to the hotel lobby.

She'd thought it proper to rush inside a moment and check her makeup and hair before the press took their pictures. She had to look sharp, smart—respectable. Show the world that no, she wasn't a slut, and she wasn't the clouds-for-brain careless mother Hector had painted her for, either.

She'd been eager to discover if David had come.

But she didn't see her boy. She didn't even make it to the ladies room.

Instead, she found Hector.

Correction: Hector found her.

Her blood froze. She felt his presence at five feet like an open assault on her person, there was such antipathy in the air.

He just stood there, blond and blue-eyed in the cool, calm moonlight. People always used to think he was her brother. But no. He was a monster. A polite, cold-hearted monster.

He'd taken things from her he shouldn't have taken, abused her in mental and emotional ways she should never have allowed, trampled her innocence, her self-respect. *Do you know how to do anything except stand there looking pretty, Beth? Are you goddamned stupid?*

Bethany had sucked it up, because that is what her mother had taught her to do. "Beth, if your father didn't like the eggs, I'd suck it up and make him new ones. Suck it up, baby, I didn't raise whiners in this house."

Except with Hector it wasn't the eggs. It was how Beth ran the house with a free hand, how she put their child in danger if he licked his hands and ate germs from the supermarket cart. It was everything about Beth.

Her father had been strict and her mother had sucked it up. But her mother had received love and praise from her husband, too, while Beth had received nothing. Months after a lavish wedding and a hopeful "I take thee," Beth had found herself a shell of a person, glancing at women out in the street and envying how carefree they looked, how independent.

Beth had forgotten how to laugh for her kid.

By the day she packed her and David's bags and left Hector, she'd spent months building up her self-esteem, gathering the remains of what had once been a person and trying to become someone again. A mother.

Even *that* he'd taken away from her.

Now they faced each other, and she wasn't sure who appeared more stunned. They'd spotted each other in the same instant. His mouth parted. She expected something would come out of it, but for a moment nothing did.

He took in her appearance—the dress Landon had provided at the last minute. Elegant and midnight blue, it made her skin seem smooth as porcelain and her eyes more electric.

Her heart beat one, two, three times.

Hector's doctorly face—the one he used to persuade his patients to do whatever he told them to because he, in fact, was a god—failed him. His mouth clamped shut and color rushed up to his face, as though the sight of her—alive and looking well—infuriated him. He took a step.

"You're marrying Gage." The sneer lashed at her like a whip crack, and she hated that she instinctively flinched, panicked into immobility.

"You're marrying Gage and you expect me to let you see our son? Why did you call him? You're forbidden to talk to him. You're forbidden to see him, or have you forgotten?"

Confrontation. God, she hated this.

Not here, *not here*.

Beth glanced around the patio, and when she saw

nothing but shadows, her chest constricted with foreboding.

No one was within hearing range, unless she screamed.

But with reporters here?

She didn't want to. She hadn't screamed the time she'd found a hairy tarantula in her kitchen, and she wouldn't scream now.

Oh, God, taking in the sight of his boyish, pretty face, she couldn't believe she could be disgusted by any living being so much. Not even cockroaches.

In the space of six years, this man had managed to turn a healthy human being into a puddle of fear, a nobody, a robot, and even now as she stared at him, she felt that fear, that anger, that despair that he had her son with him and she didn't.

He had everything.

But she had Landon.

Struggling to tame her emotions at that thought, she eased back a step, but that only made him move forward. Hector seethed with palpable anger, while fury and hurt churned inside her belly. *He took my little boy from me.* Her voice sharpened. "David is as much my son as he is yours." How dare Anna tell him she'd called? How dare he take David away from her? How dare they?

"And you're not seeing him again, I'll make sure of that!"

Blasted by the frigidness of his words, she could do nothing as he caught her elbow before she could run and yanked her forward, his serpent's hiss thrust into her ear.

"If you ever, ever, tell Gage anything about me or my practice…"

With a breath-clogging twist, Beth wrenched free and cried mutinously, "What? What are you going to do?"

"You don't want to know, Beth, but I assure you, you'll wish you hadn't opened your mouth to speak."

A gust of wind lashed at her, kicking up strands of her hair. She pushed them back and glanced around one more time, frantically now, unable to help wishing Landon could see her. Hell, she almost wished his dogs were here, flanking her. She'd never thought she'd be so happy to see two beasts like that near her person before, but the relief she felt thinking of the bodily harm they could inflict on Hector made her suddenly love that pair.

"If you put a hand on David," she warned with renewed courage, her nails biting into her hands as she clenched her fists.

"I don't need to put a hand on him to hurt him

and you know it. I'll just tell him the truth about his mother and see how he likes it."

"Lies, all lies!" Nearly bursting with rage, Beth edged backward, wanting to flee.

"I'm not alone now, Hector," she said, sucking in a calming breath. His eyes flared slightly and Beth remembered Hector saying how much he'd relish destroying the Gages. Well, she wouldn't let him! "Landon is much more powerful than you are," she informed him proudly. "And he won't rest until David's back where he belongs."

She didn't know if Hector believed her, but in her panic-ridden thoughts, she prayed he did and put a cork on his threats already. This didn't have to get so bloody. For David's sake, in fact, she wished she could come to a satisfying arrangement in the most quiet way possible—but she knew her new husband deserved better. He deserved his revenge.

And she was so starved for Hector's blood, she wanted him to get it.

"You're mine, Beth." Hector hissed out the poisonous words. "I'm here, right here." He knocked his head with his knuckles, hard. "You're weak, and I've got you, I *control* you, and I will have you again, you will come crawling back to me, mark my words."

With that, Hector spun around and walked away.

Her eyes burned as she watched his retreating back until everything in her line of vision became a blur. The encounter left her limp. She fell in a pool of her own skirts, and sat back against the wall of the building.

"God," she shakily gasped, suddenly covering her face in her hands. How could a person you hated so much have given you the thing you most loved in the world?

"Say, Gordon, where did my daughter run off to?"

"Landon," he said to his new mother-in-law, a chirpy, sunny woman with a confused, tremulous smile. "And I'll find her, Mrs. Lewis, give me a moment."

The woman appeared bemused as to what he'd said and nodded twice. She really *was* deaf.

Depositing her with Beth's father, who currently got acquainted with Julian John, Landon scoured the gardens and opted to check the least trafficked entry to the lobby. The press was getting restless. They wanted their money shot and the success of their plan depended on Landon to deliver.

He found her lying on the ground by the side of the long building. He spotted the midnight blue skirts of her dress first pooled all around her, her hair covering her profile as she mumbled angrily to herself.

He halted in his tracks. "Bethany?"

Her head snapped back. "Landon." The breath *whooshed* out of her.

He felt a sliver of dread at the sight of her pale face, as pale as the moonlight, her eyes as round as the moon but dark and terrified.

"What are you doing?" he asked uneasily, stalking forward and dropping on his haunches.

Bethany craned her neck back to meet his gaze. Her smile lacked conviction. "Hey," she said in a quavery voice, then she sighed and rubbed her face with unsteady hands. "I was feeling miserable all by myself."

Landon was at a loss. He knew how to deal with his mother—a blunt, forthright woman who'd borne three sons and had survived a husband who'd put any alpha to shame. But Beth…she was so rigid and so wound up, fighting so hard to stand when her life had crumpled around her, he just didn't know what to say to her. He couldn't explain how easily he understood this, understood that she was looking for herself, for her strength, while at the same time searching desperately for a light at the end of the tunnel.

He reached out and covered one milky white hand

with his, awkwardly at first, shocked by his body's instant reaction to such a simple touch. "You okay?"

Hell, it had been too long since he touched anyone. Too long since he'd wanted to make this sort of contact, this contact he enjoyed making with Beth. Her shoulders sagged as she gripped his fingers, and a jolt of her scent made his nostrils flare. Lemons. God, she smelled so good he found himself leaning closer for another whiff.

"Hector was just here," she said, squeezing his hand.

His hackles raised, every muscle in his body clenching. "Where?"

Beth sighed drearily while thoughts of Halifax slammed into Landon's mind, one after the other. Halifax being seen by the press…Halifax meeting in secret with Beth, swiftly and efficiently ruining the new, respectable image Landon planned for his fiancée.

His grip tightened so hard Beth winced. "Beth, where?"

"He's gone, I think."

He released her. But a swift, overwhelming anger surged inside him like a tidal wave, and his mind clamored for him to do some serious damage to that weasel. Halifax could spoil everything. He could ruin their pretend engagement, make the press believe she was still a treacherous Jezebel and that now she'd found a new target: Landon.

It was a hard sell, but not impossible.

Nothing was impossible for a twisted mind like Halifax's.

Christ, the man begged for it. And Landon was aching to give him what he deserved. Not here, not tonight, but the bastard had had it coming for a long, long time, and now the clock was ticking. Tick, tock, tick, tock.

The man had the balls to waltz into his engagement party and exchange words with his bride—just like he'd had the balls years ago to sleep with his wife.

Landon breathed out through his nose, attempting to focus, control his rage. Belatedly he noticed Beth's bewilderment and felt his gut clench.

Searching for something to say other than the twisted things he wanted to do to the man, he gently stroked the top of her shiny blonde head with his hand, curving his palm around her skull and drawing her gaze to his. He had to do something, say something to comfort her. "Here I thought you'd met my mother." He felt his lips curl upward.

She made a sound, like a laugh, then regarded him as if he'd just become a giant scorpion. "Landon, maybe this wasn't such a good idea. Us…marrying…"

He shot her a get-serious look, then seized her chin in one hand and searched her gaze. A wrenching sensation slammed into his midsection. "Maybe I underestimated you," he murmured. "You have feelings for him."

"I have hate!"

"Then *use* it! Hang on to it, Bethany. Your hate will feed mine. You want me to be ruthless, don't you?"

"Yes."

"You want me to have no heart? To trample him to the ground?"

"Yes."

"Do you want your child back?"

"Of course I do!"

"Smile then—and get out there with me. Let the reporters have a good look at my future wife." He helped her to her feet, gritting his teeth as he felt his body respond when her breasts brushed against his chest on her way up.

She wiped at her face and straightened her shoulders, amazing him with how easily she composed herself. "I'm sorry, I'm not usually so emotional."

"Hold your head high."

"Okay."

"Hold my hand."

Her palm felt cool when she slipped it inside his, and he gave it a squeeze as he guided her around the corner. She walked easily beside him, but a hint of alarm still lingered in her voice. "Landon, I feel like all these people can see right through me. That they know this is a farce and that I have no clue who you are. I mean, do you like sports? Do you take your coffee black or—?"

"I like sports. And I like strong coffee."

"I have mine with milk, two Splendas and cream."

"Do me a favor, Beth?"

"What?"

"Just act like you love me."

Six

Blinding camera lights exploded as they approached.

Beth put all her efforts into her smile and struggled to remember *why* she needed to fool all of these people. *Look fabulous, Beth, look besotted, ecstatic,* she thought, *so ecstatic a judge won't resist granting custody of David to such a dazzling couple.*

Landon was greeting the press in a congenial tone when a brazen reporter elbowed himself forward, mike in hand. "Miss Lewis—how does your ex-husband feel about the wedding?"

Beth had not been prepared for that question. She and Landon had reviewed some facts in the car when she'd asked him for instructions on dealing with the press, and he'd said, "Whatever you do, don't lie. Twist the truth however you want, but don't lie, not to them. One lie will take your credibility, and then you'll never get it back."

Very admirable and smart of him. But now she glanced worriedly at Landon and saw that he smiled at the group, an arrogant lilt of his lips that made his eyes turn to ice.

"If the good doctor's smart about it, he'll wish us well," he said, and with a nod, signaled to another reporter in a move that granted him the next question.

"Miss Lewis, how did you two meet?"

She spoke quickly, grateful at how easy the answer came. "We met at a benefit. Just one peek at this man and I was done for." Landon smiled at her, and her stomach tumbled.

"Mr. Gage, after so many years a widowed bachelor, why marry now?"

Landon's sudden frown indicated he thought the questioner may, just may, be a little bit stupid.

After allowing this reaction to sink in among the reporters, he spread an arm out toward Beth. "Take a good look at her, gentlemen, and tell me what healthy red-blooded American male wouldn't be honored to have this woman at their side?"

Hoots and a "Right on, Landon!" spread across the group, and a few other questions came up, to which he and Beth easily responded. Did he think she was beautiful? When she was young, she'd been thought beautiful by boys. But now? After Hector?

A few other questions came her way, and Beth tried to keep the mood light and happy, following Landon's cue and wry jokes. Then Landon nodded at a young man she'd heard was a famous celebrity/social-scene blogger.

"Any hints on where you'll be honeymooning?" the man asked.

"Somewhere quiet," Landon replied with a cool smile, and another round of flashes exploded.

"Mrs. Gage, how do you feel about the wedding?"

This time the microphone was held out to Landon's mother, who stood a few feet behind them, and Beth's spirits sunk. Her future mother-in-law would hate her. What woman who witnessed their son being dragged to war wouldn't?

They'd been introduced just hours ago and Beth had felt like the proverbial bug under the woman's silver-handled loupe. But Mrs. Gage had class, and she said with a regal tilt of her head, "I'm thrilled to have another woman in the family. We haven't had much time to talk, but I can already tell Beth and I have a lot in common."

Like what? Landon? Beth wondered.

A reporter next turned to Garrett. "How about

you, Garrett, any thoughts on your new sister-in-law?"

Garrett made a mischievous face that sparked up an attractive glint in his eye. "Regret that Lan saw her first."

The reporters laughed, and Beth jumped in, suddenly inspired. "Actually, *I* spotted him first."

Landon smiled at her, pulled her close to his side, and her stomach went crazy again. Within moments, Landon waved the press off, insisting they end the session. "Last shot, guys."

"How about a kiss from the couple."

He ignored the suggestion and let them take another round of pictures, still holding her, but only lightly.

"Kiss her, Mr. Gage," another reporter encouraged.

He smiled sharply, and swiftly handed her a glass of champagne—and they drank to more flashes.

Though they both continued to smile, something sizzled between them.

Beth heard a chorus of requests begin and hated how silly, how *predictable,* how absurd it was to be asked to kiss someone you really had no reason to be kissing.

The chorus rose to a crescendo all of a sudden,

deafening her clamoring heartbeat. "Kiss her! Kiss her! Kiss her!"

Her color rose as Landon took her champagne flute and set it aside. "Well, Beth."

It was inevitable.

"If there are any doubts left, we might as well dispel them."

Of course, she should take one for the team, do this for David...

The pressure of his fingers on her back brought her one step closer to him. Their eyes met. He smiled down at her, but his gaze held a warning. A request to comply.

His eyes were heat and flames; black coals burning. *It's all for show, all for show*—Beth recited the thought like a mantra—*sliding your hand into his, your legs turning to syrup, not remembering why you're here, it's all for show.*

She suppressed a tremble as he ducked his head, still smiling.

She wanted to smile like him, but couldn't. It was an act, it had to be, how she parted her lips and waited for his mouth. He breathed in her ear. "Easy."

She wanted to melt.

The way he concentrated on her mouth made her go hot.

Their lips touched. His brushed over hers at first,

a wistful, feathery touch that sent her control careening down a precipice she feared she'd never recover. She held her breath until her lungs burned and found her fingers digging into his shoulders.

He didn't have to put his hands, warm and strong, on the sides of her face as he kissed her.

He didn't have to smell like he did, or brush her lips so exquisitely.

He didn't have to slide his tongue inside, but he did.

Desire hit her like a cannon blast, making her legs tremble. She gripped him harder and he slanted his head, in command as his mouth closed over hers, taking hers, leading. Wow, he deserved an Oscar. She believed that kiss to be as real as the reporters believed it, as real as her skyrocketing pulse. It wasn't a messy kiss, it was soft, long and warm, and it was heartbreaking.

Because she'd wanted it since the moment she'd seen him come to her rescue after the Hector debacle. She'd wanted it since he'd helped her to her feet, his body a fortress of strength and warmth. She'd wanted it since the first reporter suggested they kiss and he'd pretended ignorance.

God, maybe she'd wanted it forever.

He didn't end the kiss abruptly, but quietly, his mouth lingering over hers, as though still not ready to detach, their breaths mingling as, inch by inch, he drew back. She almost moaned, her lips burned, her body burned, the heights of need to which he'd sent her unimaginable.

Slowly, Landon adjusted their stance, shifting so that she covered his hardness with her rear.

Noticing she was flustered, he waved a commanding hand at the press. "Enough. That's enough pictures tonight."

The flashes stopped. Photographers stepped back a few paces, but Landon didn't allow Beth the same luxury; his big hand rested on her hip proprietarily. His fingers bit into her skin, keeping her against him.

When the reporters dispersed, Beth wiggled free, avoiding his gaze, then snatched another champagne glass and went behind the safety of a twisting oak. Cloaked in shadows, she slumped against the tree trunk and blinked into the darkness.

How could a man kiss like that? She'd felt stroked all over, indecently stroked. She'd never been so aware of having such sensitive, eager nipples.

She kept telling herself that having sex with him would be a bad idea, a risky venture, one where if she ended up pregnant, he'd take her child just like Hector had. But even as her mind raced with protests, the other side of her brain already formulated a list of ways to avoid pregnancy while bringing their passion to fruition.

Damn. How was she supposed to say no to a guy who kissed like a volcanic avalanche?

She exhaled a breath she'd been holding, tightened her hold on her glass. She felt…helpless. Resented having to give him any kisses. It had been difficult last night at the hotel in her awkward attempts to enlist him, and it had been more so now that they'd been watched. She didn't want to know his taste and now, well, now she'd never be able to forget it.

"You handled yourself well."

Startled, she spotted her mother-in-law a few feet away. The woman wore an emerald green dress and a string of pearls, and her smile beamed with approval.

In the face of all that dignity and Texan charm, Beth forced herself to straighten, smoothing her hands along her hips. "I'm not new to the newspaper scene. It's just nice to be treated with respect for a change."

A chilly breeze sent the skirts of their dresses fluttering. "Then let me give you a piece of advice, Beth." She jerked her chin in the press's direction. "You win those people's hearts, and you win the world."

Beth narrowed her eyes, confused by this bit of

wisdom. She'd been swept into Landon's golden, glittering world of silk and velvet and music tonight—and they were lies, all lies, all for one purpose only.

Didn't the woman know?

"Landon's already doing that," she then replied, cautiously. "Winning their hearts and the world."

She gazed out at the gardens that led to the parking lot. They were vast and beautiful but they were shrouded in darkness. Dark and beckoning like Landon.

Past her shoulder, she spotted him, polite and easy as he talked to some of the reporters. He was such a solid, dynamic man, every time she saw him she found herself holding her breath.

"Why you, I wonder."

That comment snapped Beth around. There wasn't antagonism in her voice but genuine curiosity glimmered in her soft gray eyes.

"Me?"

"Well…" A jeweled hand fluttered in the air. "He's been a bachelor for six years, and a lot of women have tried to get him. Why you?"

"I don't want him, Mrs. Gage, and he doesn't want me. We just happen to want the same thing."

Spying on Landon once more, she watched him sip his drink as he assessed his surroundings.

"Maybe that's why…" she added, to herself.

The woman huffed. "My son doesn't need anyone to take down any man."

Beth nodded, then thought of the little black book, of their prenup, their upcoming marriage. There was more at stake for her than for him. Why did he agree to marry her? Because he hates him, too, she thought. Her stomach contracted at the thought of all that Landon had lost because of Hector. "We won't last," she said out loud, unable to take her eyes off her betrothed.

Hector criticized the press, but Landon respected them and was clearly admired in return. Hector had hated that about him. Landon needed only to stand there, be cordial, treat them like human beings, not bend to them or try desperately to be liked by them, and they adored him. Whereas Hector used to bribe them.

"Have you met Kate?" Eleanor's voice filtered through her thoughts.

Beth spotted a young redhead heading in their direction. She radiated so much energy, she could've been a little sun. Her lopsided smile had trouble-maker written all over it.

Beth liked her instantly.

"I'm the caterer," Kate said, offering a tray. "And you're Beth. Hi, Beth."

"Kate is also a friend of the family." The affection in her mother-in-law's words was also visible in her gracefully aged face.

"*Almost* family," Kate corrected as she picked up an hors d'oeuvre from her own tray. She winked conspiratorially at Beth. "I'm going to marry Julian. Poor guy doesn't know it yet."

Beth glanced in Julian's direction, but her gaze never reached him. Her eyes snagged on Garrett, who watched Kate as she tasted her creation.

"Umm. Delicious, if I do say so myself," Kate said, and smiling, licked her fingers before a riveted Garrett.

She was playing a game, Beth realized. A game of jealousy. Kate waved at Garrett, smiling to him, and Beth could see the expression in Garrett's face, tight with displeasure and heated with lust.

She thought about warning her of playing games with these men, with a Gage, but then bit back the thought. For wasn't she in league with a Gage? And weren't they, too, playing a game? Kissing, for crying out loud. With tongues. There absolutely had to be no more kissing—her son was at stake. Her entire future!

"Why are you all being so nice to me?" she asked Kate when her mother-in-law became engaged with another couple, for Kate seemed like someone who spoke the blunt, unfiltered truth. Honestly, if she were Landon's mother and a strange woman had asked him to marry her in a week, for any reason, she'd want to smack both the woman and her son.

But Kate patted her shoulder. "We're nice because you're *good* for Lan."

"Me? See, now you have no idea what you're saying."

She'd proposed a bloody game of revenge—she'd become some sort of vengeful witch. Courtesy of some sleazy bastard.

Kate propped a shoulder against the oak tree. "The truth is the last few years have been painful for the family, seeing Landon like he's been." Beth's gaze drifted to the tall, breathtaking man currently dismissing the reporters. "He's always been the head, and when he's so quiet, so…unfeeling, well, there's tension, you know? All he did was work and work and work, and that's not healthy."

Both women's gazes were drawn to him. Landon turned his head to look at Beth, and as they stared, the corner of his lips twitched. She saw a glimmer of victory in his eyes, shining with satisfaction, as he slowly lifted his champagne glass to her in celebration. The press had bought it. The kiss, the engagement. They'd bought it.

Beth smiled back at him, lifting her own glass in a distant toast.

Partners in crime.

God, she loved having him on her side!

He loved the way she kept scouting the crowd for him.

Hell, he loved the way she kept trying not to smile at him.

And the way she'd melted, like pudding, when she'd kissed him.

"You do realize you're smiling. Right, Lan?"

Landon tore his gaze from Beth and drained the last of his champagne flute. He'd been smiling? Like some idiot? He hadn't realized. His mind had been spinning all night, plotting, planning. There was still no unleashing of his anger, and then the lust that had come afterward, with Beth's kiss. "Halifax was here," he told Garrett.

"What—tonight?"

"Son of a bitch talked to Beth."

"Can you trust her, Landon?"

Landon stole another glance at her, one of many this evening. He needed to think with his head.

"I should post someone on her."

"What about that detective who brought you all the dish on Chrystine and Halifax?"

"Is he still the best?"

"I think so, yes." Garrett's eyes, black as coals from their father's side, narrowed thoughtfully. "Why would you want someone on her tail?"

Landon frowned into his glass, surprised to find it empty. "My own peace of mind."

"You don't think Halifax sent her to you, do you? How far can his fury run?"

He couldn't take his eyes off her, so pretty as she talked animatedly with Kate. "If it runs as far as mine then there's no telling what he'll do."

Garrett propped his shiny Italian leather boots up on a stone bench. "You can still back out, Lan. You haven't married her yet."

Yes, he could. He didn't need Beth to ruin Halifax, he knew that. But somehow, the desire for revenge just wasn't as fierce without her.

He remembered how pale she'd been moments ago, how frightened, and the thought of her getting hurt made him grit his molars. "Halifax could be more dangerous than we think."

"True." Garrett shrugged. "Then again, I still can't see why that guy hates you so much."

"Because he wanted Chrystine… They were fooling around after she had the baby—remember all those emails the detective printed out for me? Hell,

Garrett, I still can't believe Beth was married to that scumbag."

His son had died because of that bastard. Because of his selfish demands that Chrystine meet him the night of one of the worst storms on record.

The loss of that bright-eyed baby boy had almost killed Landon. No parent should have to feel it, no man, no animal, no innocent woman who'd do anything for her son.

"While I go poking into his business, I need to know Bethany's safe. If she's being followed, where she goes, what she eats."

"Has it occurred to you she and Halifax might be out to ruin you together? She may still be loyal to him. In the end, Chrystine was."

Landon pondered those words. But to compare Bethany with his first wife was unfair. Chrystine had been a social-climbing, self-centered princess, and Landon had known what she wanted from him from the start—his money, and the power his name would grant her. He hadn't planned to give her either—until she got pregnant. And to a man like him, marriage had been the only option.

Bethany, on the other hand, just wanted her kid back.

"She's my fiancée now, Garrett, and in a few days, my wife. Not his," he growled then.

His chest swelled with unexpected possessiveness at the thought.

Tonight she'd stood tall, and Landon felt damned proud of the way she'd held up during the photo session.

She'd smiled, she'd acted with class and style, and the kiss she'd delivered had been so scorching, so real, she'd left him hot and bothered and eager to stake his claim on her once and for all.

In the quiet moonlight as she chatted with Kate, Beth's face had lost its paleness and her cheeks now glowed a soft pink. She looked so pretty he worried it would...haunt him.

"You're determined to go through with the wedding."

"Yes," he said, emphatic.

"Why?"

He'd asked himself a dozen times. Why did he want to marry her?

Because she made him want revenge...because he never tired of staring into her blue, blue eyes... because there was something about Bethany, plain and simple as he'd thought she was, that just got to him. And every minute was getting to him more.

"She deserves better than this, Garrett," he said, honestly. Better than loneliness, lies and Halifax.

Across a handful of shoulders, he watched Beth-

any push a wheaten strand of hair behind her ear…
"Christ, she's so sexy." He dropped his head back in
exasperation, closing his eyes for a second. "She'll
be sleeping sixteen steps away from my bedroom
door starting tonight—I doubt I'll sleep an hour."

Garrett burst out laughing, then pounded Landon's back with one hand. "So, what are you going
to do about it?" he asked.

Patience, Landon thought. Cold showers and more
patience.

"You've never romanced a single woman in your
life. They all came to you, just like Beth did."

"Obviously, Bethany's different." She didn't want
him. Did she? She needed time.

She was a woman rediscovering herself, taking
her first steady steps to seize the things she wanted.
And Landon needed, had to make sure, that those
steps lead her to *him*.

He caught her watching from afar, her eyes shining with excitement. Then she gave him one of those
shy, we've-got-them smiles.

Slowly, he returned it. While he did, his heart
boomed loudly, his blood stirred, and his mind was
pulled in all kinds of directions which led to the
same end.

Beth, in bed, with Landon.

"You know what I think?" Garrett offered, though

God knows Landon hadn't asked for his opinion. "I think you're falling."

Landon grimly shook his head.

"You're falling."

He tipped his glass up to his lips, but when no liquid came forth, he snatched a new glass from a passing waiter. "Negative, little brother. I'm merely interested."

He thought of the torment of romancing her, night after night, watching her defenses crack, one by one, and his insides turned to fire. Yes. He'd do it gradually, so methodically she wouldn't even realize how fiercely he wanted her….

"You're not seducing her already, and that's not like you. Why isn't she in your bed? I'm telling you. You're falling."

"Garrett?"

Garrett continued to nod direly. "Falling big-time, bro."

"Shut up, moron."

But his brother had a point here, a very valid point.

If he wasn't careful, he was going to fall for his own fake wife before he'd even bedded her.

Seven

Score one point for the avengers.

And zero for the pig.

Beth was humming the next morning, she was so pleased about last night.

She hummed during her shower, she hummed as she brushed her hair, she hummed as she selected the shoes she would wear—a pair of classic Mary Janes—and mentally planned all the test recipes she would be posting on Kate's new website.

Kate had mentioned wanting to expand her catering business, create a blog, menus, an online site. Last night Beth had asked Landon to borrow one of his computers and had delved into the task with the sight of being able to do something from home, when she regained custody of David.

So Beth had stayed up late last night, inspired and invigorated, because things were changing.

More than just her residence had changed.

Beth was different. She was taking charge of her life—she was getting David back.

And this time, she was going to keep him forever.

Landon, however, was not humming when she spotted him downstairs. He was on the phone, his tone crisp.

"In an hour. At the office. Right. I want him on the job starting today."

He hung up. Beth said, "Good morning."

She went to the coffeemaker on the buffet table, scooping grounds into a basket. Then assessed him from the corner of her eye as she waited for the coffee to start trickling.

He looked so sharp. In a black suit and tie, clean-shaven, his dark hair still damp from a recent shower and slicked back to reveal his hard-boned face. Lord, he was striking. But this morning... brooding somehow.

His hands were thrust inside his pockets, but Beth wasn't fooled by the casualness of that pose. Upon further inspection, she realized his expression was positively morose.

Puzzled, she took a seat at a small round game

table, and Landon surveyed her with slitted eyes. What was up with him today?

"Did I miss something?" she asked, frowning.

He made a noncommittal sound, as though whatever he'd been about to say couldn't quite be said, and shook his head like the situation was dire.

His expression made Beth's unease increase tenfold. *"What?"*

"Who told Halifax of the engagement party? You?"

Her hands began to shake so hard, she set down her coffee mug before she spilled it all over herself. Something tumultuous charged the air. Landon looked…enraged. "I called David, remember? You said I could invite him."

"And who did you speak to? Hector?"

She frowned in consternation and her stomach churned uncomfortably. "Anna, the housekeeper. She's become a nanny to him, I think. Why? Why do you have that look on your face?"

He reached for the sofa, then flung a newspaper for her to see. "The picture today in every newspaper except the *Daily* is not ours. It's of Halifax."

Beth gasped as she spotted Hector's loathed face staring back at her from the black and white picture. "No!"

The headline was even more disgusting than Hector.

Gage and Lewis engaged in illicit affair long before wedding date...

"Yeah," he said, tightly, and slammed his fist into the table. "Hell, yeah."

Panic bubbled up inside her. "God! You're the owner of a newspaper, can't you do something?"

"Beth, it wasn't just the *Daily* covering the party, it was the *Houston Chronicle*, the *Dallas Morning News*, even the *Enquirer*, for God's sake."

"And that is my fault, how?" Beth pushed her chair back, the outrage that swept her so intense her voice trembled. "I'm sorry it didn't go as we planned but that certainly wasn't me. And you full well know we're not—you and I are not having... having sex."

His pointed stare and the way it slowly raked up and down her body made her nipples bead so wickedly under her buttoned shirt she wanted to hide. "No, Beth, you and I are not having sex yet."

Her blood bubbled in her veins. What did he mean by *yet?* "Landon, it was a mistake to call David. I see that now. But he's just a little boy. All I wanted was to see him."

But Landon rammed a finger to his temple and

made a twisting motion. "Emotions make us sloppy, Beth. You need a cool head."

"How can I when my son is with that monster!"

Crossing the distance between them, he seized her shoulders and leveled their gazes, as if that alone could make her see the problem through his glimmering silver eyes. "Precisely why you can't risk our position." God, his stunning features were so much more amazing up close, she could barely decipher his words. "You can't attempt to see David anymore, not until I say so—I can't have you saying or doing the wrong thing around Halifax. It could compromise everything. Understand me?"

"I understand."

He released her. "All right," he relented, dropping his arms. "So not a word to Halifax unless our lawyer is present—agreed, Bethany?"

"Why on earth are you snapping at me, I'm on your side!"

"Just stay away from Halifax from now on." He grabbed the newspapers scattered throughout and rammed them into his briefcase before locking it shut. "I've got to go."

"You forgot this one." She glowered down at the paper as though she could destroy it with one glare. God, it was so not what they'd planned, she wanted to hit someone. "What are we supposed to do now?"

she asked him as he took the paper from her. Their fingers brushed and sent a disquieting little tingle through her arm.

The kiss. Oh God, she'd almost mated with him right there in front of everybody, and for nothing. For more lies, more and more lies from Hector.

Landon started for the foyer, all angry power and dark predatory steps. "We do what we planned to do. We're getting married."

The front door slammed shut.

For Beth, the next few days were busy.

They consisted of overseeing the run of the household along with the housekeeper, Martha; working on her and Kate's project; worrying about David and cursing that loathed, cheating, bribing snake Hector; wondering what Landon was doing and when he would get home and if he would smile at her; then back to Kate and Beth's project.

Her new friend was thrilled to have Beth help with her catering business. She'd used the word "brilliant" to qualify Beth's Gourmet for Kids idea; fancy recipes for kids like stacked chicken fingers over a bed of fries. Just knowing Kate thought the idea could work, and that if it did, Beth would be able to do it from home, thrilled her.

She'd asked Kate if they could offer recipes on the

site for free and make money offering advertising, and Kate had given her carte blanche on it.

The website was still under construction, but Beth was pouring all of her creativity into the design down to every last detail, even making sure that while a customer navigated the site, a cute little carrot appeared rather than a mouse arrow.

And Landon. Well, that man was enough to keep a woman on her toes. He drilled Beth about Hector, more determined than ever to find out the skeletons in that beast's closet. Beth had, by some miracle of nature, been able to resist handing over the black book yet. Just to make sure that he had enough incentive to marry her.

It was hard not to yearn for his company when he went to work, though. He was a greedy Monopoly player, a ruthless chess player, and he loved to steal her out at night for a ride in one of the cars from his collection. He drove well beyond the speed limit at midnight when there was little traffic.

Her traitorous heart leapt every time he walked into a room and flashed her that smile of his and called her Bethany. Oh, he was suave, that one was.

Did Hector think he won after bribing the press after their engagement party? Ha! That would not be the case with the judge. *Not this time, pig.*

She grinned at her reflection and tried that out loud. "Not this time, pig!"

Yes, it felt awesome.

It was past evening now. The eve of their wedding.

Landon was still at the *Daily* as usual, and Beth stood before a vanity and oval mirror in her simple silken wedding dress. Why she'd thought it important to try it on again, she didn't dare dwell on.

The dress was sexier than she remembered, she thought as she critically studied herself. It hugged her body in an enticing way. The cut, though demure, somehow still managed to be modern and attractive, and the flattering cream color made her sort of...

"Stunning."

She stiffened at the male voice, then caught sight of Landon's piercing regard in the mirror's reflection. The color crawled up her cheeks. "It's bad luck for the groom to see the bride in her wedding dress," she said.

Nothing moved. Time, the world, had paused when Landon arrived.

Swallowing awkwardly, Beth turned and shrugged. "But I guess we're getting divorced, so..."

He remained motionless, a sentinel blocking the door.

His eyes glowed. So, so slowly, they wandered

over her body, head to toe, and they glimmered with such heat they scorched every inch of her they covered.

The form-fitting dress with the high neckline suddenly felt as transparent as a spider's web.

She bit her lip, unable to stifle the shudder that coursed through her. "It feels glued—" she pulled at the satin on her hips "—to my skin." All of a sudden.

"The only thing glued to your skin are my eyes." His voice was husky, and Beth's thighs liquefied. Ducking her head, she unclipped her hair and used it to create a waterfall so he couldn't see her blush.

His words...hurt. The way he looked at her. Hurt.

Maybe because she was starting to admire and respect him. And because he was amazing and sexy and kissable and staring at her with those bedroom eyes all the time, and she couldn't stand it.

Her insides knotted, and she closed her eyes and covered her face with her hands, smothering a groan. "Can you please get out of here, Landon? You're making me nervous."

She kept her eyes shut and strained her ears to hear him leave. Hopefully, he'd close the door behind him, too. But for a charged moment nothing in the room seemed to move.

Her heart stopped when she heard a footstep,

and a second, and a third. To her alarm, they were coming in her direction. Suddenly, Landon stood too close. His familiar scent penetrated her lungs, making them want to explode.

His arms, strong and hard, slowly slid around her waist. A fluttery, hopeful sensation danced inside her and she couldn't quite quell it. He murmured her name over the top of her head as he drew her to his strong body.

Feeling naked and vulnerable in his arms, she dropped her hands to his shoulders—in a poor, poor effort to push him away—but didn't dare open her eyes.

What was he doing?

Why had he stared at her as if she were naked?

God, what was he *doing?*

"Look at me," he said.

She bit her trembling lower lip and quietly refused to.

His hand slid languorously up her spine, and his fingers caressed the bare skin on her back as he huskily murmured, "Look at me, Beth…"

She felt the gentle cup of his hand on the back of her head, drawing her forward until his lips were a breath away.

"…and tell me you don't want this."

He covered her lips with his. She stiffened at the

contact, trying to fight it, but his lips felt plush and warm, and when the wet silk of his tongue swept into her mouth, she was lost. Lost in the moment, in a kiss that was profound with yearning and rough with hunger, a kiss that was shattering and devastating and beautiful, a kiss from a man she wanted and feared and admired.

An unfamiliar desperation rose inside her, the need to experience this closeness with someone staggering in intensity, making her not only respond but do so with hot, ardent abandon. Whoever he was, whatever he was, he was suddenly more crucial than air, and her every defense against him fled. Her fingers bit into his shoulders and her mouth began to move frantically under his.

"More," he rasped, and slanted his head, "Give me more."

A moan rushed out of her, muffled by his mouth as their lips dissolved in a hungry, wild exploration. He tasted of coffee. Smelled like a man. His hands greedily roamed her sides, along her back, clutching and kneading even while pressing her against him.

Eager to investigate every plane, ridge, angle of his body, she let her hands venture up his back and curled her fingers around his thick nape. His arms tightened around her and he groaned into her mouth. He was so aroused! She could feel it, the thundering in his chest against her breast, the sharp shudder that rushed through him as he deepened the kiss and ground his need against her in slow, suggestive moves of his hips.

Rather than fill her with fear, the stab of his broad, unyielding hardness sent a flood of warmth across her body, and the muscles of her tummy clenched with need.

In the darkness of this bedroom and very late at night, she'd wondered if he spent sleepless nights like she had, thinking of him. If he was haunted by the kiss they'd shared before the press. And if he'd both been waiting for and wanting a new one. But it was insane!

Squirming, she pushed him away and gasped for air. He pulled back, and her chest heaved crazily, and her lips tingled with the sweet moisture of his mouth.

He cupped her face between both his hands and focused on her eyes with a heavy-lidded gaze. "I won't apologize," he said, a warning.

Dizzied, Beth had trouble pulling away, couldn't seem to find her grounding. She found herself clinging to his collar with her fists. "Why? Why did you kiss me?"

There were no reporters now, no priest demanding he kiss the bride, no need to kiss her at all. She'd done the same to him that first night, but she'd been desperate. What about him?

He didn't answer. Instead, he gently pried her cramped fingers from his shirt, set her arms at her sides with a brotherly pat, and smiled a devil's smile from the door. "Good night, Bethany."

He could still taste her.

It amused him. It annoyed him. It made him feel *starved.*

Across the room, Landon watched the blonde, blue-eyed vision in a cream wedding dress mingle among the well-dressed crowd and colorful blur of dancers.

They'd planned a small celebration—nothing too posh. Bethany had asked for simple and simple was what Bethany got.

Lush white casablancas populated his home today. They were accompanied by music, candles and a promising buffet. A buffet that couldn't possibly satisfy Landon's hunger. No, nothing could appease this hunger. This aching, growing void for more.

The tension between them had been building during the week. Like a fire stoked with their plotting, their glances, their smiles. Landon was known as a patient man, but his body didn't listen to patience tonight.

He thrummed with desire. Had strained against his pants all through the ride to city hall. He'd watched her loose honeyed hair brush against her shoulders, her small, pert breasts rise and fall under her form-fitting dress.

It would have taken nothing to lean over and kiss her again. This time touch her, caress her soft skin, wrap his hands around her hair.

But she wasn't ready. Last night she'd pushed him away. And Landon would wait. So she trusted him, respected him. Wanted him bad enough to come to him.

His wife…

The tantalizing thought made him groan low in his throat. Did she moan when she made love? Did the thought of being legally bound to him play with her libido the same way it did with his? He closed his eyes and exhaled a ragged breath, attempting to forget the way her mouth had tasted, of apples and pears.

With effort, he pushed away from the limestone column in the foyer and made his way back into the party, watching Kate and Bethany chat. Her dress molded to her slender body, and the sight drove him up the wall.

Bethany spotted him, said something to Kate, then both women, Kate with her tray which she seemed hard-pressed to set down, and Beth with a smile, began coming forward.

People circulated around the living room and the small dance floor, but the noise of them went distant, unimportant somehow.

Because Beth and Kate were coming over.

His pulse went haywire.

Someone slapped his back and stopped him in his tracks. "I noticed you haven't kissed the bride," Julian said.

Garrett was with him, and the three men stood watching the women wind their way across.

"And why is that?" This from Garrett. "Last time you celebrated this very wedding, you gave us all quite a viewing, Lan."

Landon's pulse jumped as it always did when Bethany stared at him with those big bright eyes. He lowered his voice so she couldn't hear him. "It's about time I kissed her in private."

"I'm kinda put out you haven't tasted my spinach rolls," Kate said to Julian when they arrived, extending the tray.

But it was Garrett who instantly snatched one up, made an obliging sound and tasted it. Landon had seen Kate in ponytails—she was the closest to a little sister the Gages had—but it was Garrett who got five stars for sticking by her side when she grew breasts and a penchant for trouble. Poor Garrett.

"Well?" Kate prodded. "Good?"

Garrett said something, but Landon didn't hear. He hungrily studied Bethany's mouth. Her fragrance wafted into his lungs. Sweet and female, creating havoc with his insides. He didn't know what it was about her. Something intrinsic in her, the sexual siren mixed with the fierceness of a mother cougar and the calm of an angel.

"There's more where that came from," Kate said. "And there's dancing, too. You guys have heard of that, haven't you? Something people do to have fun?"

Garrett muttered something to her, yanked the tray away and shoved it into a waiter's hands, and dragged her to the dance floor. Julian took his exit cue when no one spoke a word. Bethany remained, uneasy on her feet, tucking her hair behind her ears.

Landon stepped closer, and before she could turn to leave, he reached out and seized her wrist. His voice sounded gruff even to his own ears.

"Do you want to dance?"

Oh, God, he was so sexy.

The offer—the low timbre of his voice and the

rough way he'd asked her—sent a flock of winged creatures loose inside Beth.

She nodded before she realized what she was doing and allowed Landon to lead her past Kate, past Garrett, past their families, past their friends.

They'd organized only a small celebration, had already smiled for pictures for the press. Beth had met some of Landon's Harvard friends, business colleagues. They'd done everything but dance. In fact, they'd done everything but act like a newly married couple.

Until now.

Her heart felt like a restless rabbit as they reached the farthest corner of the dance floor. Whomp whomp whomp.

This was probably just for show but the excitement swimming inside her was all too real. God, what was she going to do?

She felt his hands splay on her back and took a deep, ragged breath. The music flared and Landon drew her into the circle of his arms. The memory of the way he'd kissed her last night, the way the sight of her in this very dress had made him lose his normally sharp mind, made her stomach clench.

Striving to keep calm, she set her hands lightly on his wide shoulders and searched for chat topics in her brain but couldn't find any except one. Suddenly, that reckless kiss they'd shared had become the proverbial white elephant in the room.

The tension crackled between them, and her nerves felt like electrical wires. "You kissed me."

His eyes flashed. He tightened his hold around her, and her traitorous body molded against his lean, hard length. "I remember you kissing me back."

His rumbling voice, so near, sent little tingles racing up and down her spine, and she didn't want them to.

In a sleek black suit and silver tie, Landon was so arresting it took an enormous effort for Beth to focus on the matter at hand. Focus on anything but the rightness of being in her mock husband's arms, with those piercing thick-lashed eyes on her face.

"Landon, I wanted to speak to you about the hearing," she said.

"Beth, I don't want to talk about this now."

"But I do. I was going to bring it up tomorrow after you'd read the book but we might as well discuss it here. The sooner we get David back, the sooner we can get divorced, right?"

She just didn't trust herself not to do something stupid while married to him. Enduring his proximity every day, knowing he was near every single sleepless night, was the slowest, most painful kind of physical torture she'd ever known.

She couldn't take this much longer.

She licked her lips in nervousness. "The book's upstairs—you could probably read it in a few hours. How soon could we schedule a hearing?"

His face was indecipherable, but the firmness of his arms around her gave her the sensation of being both trapped and protected. "We need to be married for a while before I request one. And before I do, I need to make sure we'll win. I hate to say this, but you can't afford to lose again, Bethany."

She met Kate's curious gaze as she danced by with Garrett, smiled a little at her, then sighed. "It's just that every day that goes by I fear I'm losing him. What if he doesn't want me anymore? What if it's too late?"

"Your son loves you. How could he not?"

The words touched something hidden inside of her, places she dare not get into for fear of crying. She forced herself to face him. "What if he stops? What if he feels I abandoned him, what if he's told I'm a monster and he believes it? I know I can't see him but just the sight of him, to see him smile at me, that's all I want. Just to know that he…that he's still my little boy."

The tenderness in his eyes loosened a ribbon of sadness inside of her. "You feel like you disappointed him," he murmured, stroking his splayed hands up her bare back.

His warm, soothing caresses made her throat clog with emotion. "I probably did."

"You feel like you should've seen it coming, should have protected him?"

His hair had grown longer, and the silky raven black tips curled playfully at his collar. Suddenly, disturbingly, she reached upward and delved her hands into the thick silken mass. He stiffened. His hands halted. His chest vibrated as though he'd held back a groan.

Slowly, they started moving again, to the music.

She was mesmerized by the depth in his eyes, the stormy understanding, and suddenly she knew he wasn't just talking about her, not anymore. She lowered her voice, so that none of the nearby dancing couples overheard.

"You couldn't have known, either, Landon. Accidents happen."

He pulled her closer, and a muscle worked taut at the back of his jaw as he clenched it. "I could've stopped her, Beth, I heard the door, I knew there was nothing between us, I suspected she wasn't well."

She didn't realize she tenderly stroked his jaw

until she heard him breathe in, deep, as though trying to collect himself. Collect her scent.

Her nipples pricked at that sensual thought.

With a low groan, Landon turned his face into her hand and brushed his lips against the inside of her palm. "So, no, to your former question. It's not too late for you," he murmured.

His eyes held that same smoldering admiration she'd seen all week, and it made her gaze rush away and her hand return to his shoulder.

He looked hungry and compassionate and strong. Strong enough to hang on to. He was utterly gorgeous, this big bad husband of hers. Which had been creating some big bad problems for Beth.

She ached to kiss him, slide her fingers up the thick tendons at his neck, bury her face against his throat and just smell him.

"Let's not talk about it anymore," she said, quietly, then forced herself to listen to the haunting tune playing while a knot of tension continued growing in her stomach.

"You're right, let's not," he agreed.

She heard the rustle of silk as he slid his hand up her back. Her pulse quickened as his thumb grazed the bare skin.

"You enjoy…dancing?" she asked, starting to pant.

His lazy smile could disarm a regiment. "I would if you'd start moving with me."

She laughed and swayed a little more, allowing him to press her close enough to be aware of every beautiful, hard part of him. He smelled male, clean. Delicious.

His hands shifted trajectory, sliding down her back, long fingers making goose bumps prick across her bare arms.

"Mother and Kate are staying over tonight," he murmured as he studied her with scorching eyes. The deliberate brush of his fingers against the start of her buttocks made her catch her breath. "They don't want to drive at such a late hour to Alamo Heights. I'm afraid you're going to have to share my room tonight."

Her breath hitched in her lungs. The thought of being near him was hell. She feared she could resist anything, anyone, but him. *Don't don't* don't *make me lose myself, Landon.*

"What about the other room down the hall, the one—"

"That's my son's room. And it's off-limits."

His son's room. Her heart stuttered, then her eyes widened in realization. So he didn't know. He didn't know, couldn't speak that way about his son if he knew.

Pain knifed through her at the thought of knowing something so vile about his past that he didn't. He must believe that Chrystine and Hector's affair had started after he and Chrystine got married. Beth had once supposed the same, until the day she'd confronted Hector and had learned that he and the woman he was sleeping with apparently went back for years.

She loathed to think Landon didn't know that Chrystine and Hector had fooled around together before Landon even met her, and that when she ended up pregnant, Landon hadn't been the only possible father.

He'd only been the most convenient one for her purposes.

Something wrenched painfully inside her stomach at the thought of telling him. She could tell him, yes. That his first wife had been an incredible actress and a very convincing liar. But why open that wound? Why hurt him like that when he'd been wonderful to her?

God, she needed a drink. A whole lot of drinks. A margarita, a martini.

Unaware of why she'd stiffened, Landon eased his hold around her a fraction. "Relax, Bethany. I'm not going to hurt you."

She shuddered, and for one brief moment, let her

eyes drift shut and her stiffness melt away into his strength. "I know."

And Beth wasn't going to hurt him, either. Not this man. Not now, and not with this truth.

Eight

Overall, he'd say the wedding was a success.

The reporters had taken shots, most of his friends had departed, and now only family remained, lounging on the twin sofas inside the book-lined study.

Beth was on her fourth glass of champagne. Landon had consumed double that amount. She smiled now as though happy, smiling like…well, he didn't know what. But her smile was so pretty it made his lips curve, too.

"I'm thinking of something silver…" Beth's mother, Helen, said.

Everyone made their guesses, and Landon watched his wife pick the cranberries from the nut and dried fruit mix.

Note to self: she likes cranberries.

He kept wondering things, like if she slept with socks or not, if her soap smelled like she did, if she sighed when she made love, or moaned, or whimpered. He wondered if she was ticklish, and if the faraway look that sometimes shadowed her eyes was due to missing David.

He'd not wanted anything like this for years.

Unbelievable, that suddenly he was up for revenge, he was up for sex, up for seduction. Now every morning he awakened with a charge of anticipation, knowing that a woman would be under this roof with him, soon in his bed, a woman so wound up he knew she needed this as badly as he did.

"Landon, your turn."

He lifted his gaze to Kate. "My turn for…?"

"Twenty questions."

Beth's smile faded as she considered him expectantly, and a fierce tangle of desire and emotion kept getting bottled up inside him. He couldn't understand this irrational pull she had on him, but tonight he was tired of pushing against it. He scraped his chin with his thumb and forefinger, unable to think of anything.

"Something blue," he said at last.

His mother sipped her tea while his brothers started guessing, and smiling. Landon shook and shook his head. And Beth was…there were no words to describe her. That form-fitting dress looked delicious on her. He wanted to use his lips to pry it off, his teeth…

Inch by inch, the blood seemed to leave her face as he approached her, a sudden clatter of claps and cheers goading him forward. His heartbeat vibrated like thunder in his body. She inched back, buried in the sofa cushions, as he advanced.

Bending down, Landon seized her delicate chin and forced her to meet his smoldering stare. She'd been averting her gaze. Now he knew why—her eyes were welling with it. She feared this, them, the hunger between them.

"What do you think you're doing?" she murmured as he reached out to seize a handful of soft, honeyed hair. The tendrils slid like silk as they sifted between his fingers. God, he wanted to learn everything about this woman, wanted her to look at him like his mother had looked at his father before he'd died, with love and knowledge and unity.

She caught her breath when he ducked his head and, as he spoke, grazed the curved top of one ear. "My wife's eyes are blue, aren't they?"

Gently, he palmed the back of her head and dragged his mouth to cover hers. With a slight pressure of his lips, she opened, and something inside him snapped when her taste flooded him. Warm, sweet. His body went crazy for more, so he tightened his hold and let his tongue take a deep foray into her mouth. Cheers erupted around them. He had to stop, damn, he really did, but she'd just put her arms around his neck and slanted her head a bit, and, Jesus, if they'd been alone he would be tearing at her clothes, he wanted this so much.

Prolonging the moment, he deepened the kiss for just a couple of seconds longer, wanting to see if he could taste her sweet anger, hatred, passion and need inside of her. Maybe she could taste it inside of him. He tasted it all, tasted more than that. Dreams, martinis, cranberries, desire.

"I want you, Bethany," he said as he tore away and growled into her ear. "As much as I want to nail Halifax to the ground, that's how hard I want you."

He eased back, and Beth blinked up at him like she'd been ravaged without her will, and as if he'd been the bastard who'd done it. A burning need to touch her, kiss every part of her, swam through his veins. Her hair tumbled past her shoulders, her eyes were heavy and sleepy and brimming with need.

She hadn't pushed him away, and that alone knifed him with satisfaction and the need for more.

The cheers morphed into comments from his brothers, but Landon's sole attention was focused on Beth.

She seemed troubled, battling the sparks, what had been building between them. Her hands shook as she pushed herself to a stand. "I think I'm going to bed."

Landon didn't plan to remain here, being baited by his brothers, questioned by the mothers, or ribbed by Kate. He swept her up in his arms. "Good idea."

"Landon Gage, you did not just do that."

Because there was no brown bag she could cover her face with, Beth had to pretend she had hallucinated the stupefied stares of their family members as Landon carried her up the stairs. Like freaking Rhett Butler!

His steps were purposeful as he reached the landing, his jaw determined. "I think I did."

The dogs trailed close at his heels. She squirmed, worried that her poor grasp on reality was slipping. His kisses just got better and better and her breasts tingled like her lips did. "Landon, put me down."

"You're drunk, Beth."

"And?"

"And I'm going to take disgusting advantage of that." He kicked the door shut behind him and set her on her feet. Her legs felt wobbly, the room spun a little. "You have one minute to get in that bed, Bethany Gage. I'm going to kiss you senseless."

"Ha!" was all she could say. Her hands trembled as she got busy plucking at her earrings, slipping off her shoes, stealing covert glances at him as he removed his jacket, whipped off his belt. Their movements were rushed, even her awkward ones. *Rushed.*

"I can't imagine what they're all thinking!" she burst out, reaching to her side to unzip her dress. "They're going to imagine we're upstairs, doing... that."

The dogs whined out in the hall.

Landon kicked off his shoes and quickly unzipped. Bethany blinked as he pulled off his pants. He had long, hair-dusted, muscular legs and thick thighs and calves and... He was a dream. A little girl's fantasy of a prince and a little girl's fantasy of the villain, all in one man.

She couldn't do this, couldn't bear to see him. He was dreaming if he was going to kiss her senseless again. He already had, and she already feared she was losing herself in her daily fantasies of this man.

Storming into the bathroom and closet, she washed her face, slipped into the T-shirt she used as pajamas that someone—probably Martha—had brought from her room, and then she jumped on the bed, quickly sliding under the covers.

She would not look at him, and for a few seconds,

she actually succeeded. She had to cool down her jets, get herself calm and in control.

But she felt strange, a little wicked, like she had stolen a moment with her husband and that fact alone made her naughty. She turned just as he shrugged off his shirt. His chest held her mesmerized, made her lungs stop working. She'd never thought a man could be so beautiful and so virile at the same time.

She swallowed at the sight of all that bronzed flesh, the rippling muscles as he yanked the shirt off his wrists.

"I don't feel married," she blurted. "Do you?" This felt more like having an affair with the sexy town bad boy who also happened to have millions.

"Like I said, you're drunk, Beth."

She rolled to her side, giving him her back, forcing herself to stop staring at his body. "The first time I married, I cried on my wedding night," she said, because she figured talking would distract her. She didn't feel like crying now, though, she actually felt…kind of tingly and very weird.

"I'm sorry."

She swallowed. "I guess it was the moment I realized all those little romantic ideas in my head—that's all they were. Ideas, not reality."

She heard the drapes snap shut with a yank. "The first time I was married I got stone drunk."

She whipped around to face him at that. "Why?"

"Perhaps I felt cornered."

He climbed into bed in his boxers. The mattress squeaked. Her heart did something else entirely; it seemed to vault. He was practically naked under the covers, and within inches of her.

His scent wafted to her nostrils, and the butterflies in her stomach jumped and twisted as her lungs fought for air. "Cornered twice into marriage," she said, flipping around once again, hating the pulsing sensation between her legs. "I left a light on in the bathroom—it's the only way I can sleep."

He edged closer. The heat of his body singed her backside. He set a big calloused hand on her waist, and her breasts felt suddenly painful and heavy. "What are you afraid of?" he urged.

"Hector." *You.* "I slept alone most of my married life. I would lie in bed and pray he wouldn't come in, even though I felt so lonely sometimes."

His hand on her waist squeezed gently, almost possessively, and she was shocked that other parts of her body were jealous for his touch. "You don't have to sleep alone tonight."

"I love David." She shut her eyes tightly, fighting the magnetic force that seemed to be urging her to turn around and run her tongue all over his silken skin. "I think I wanted to love his father, but he makes it so difficult." *And I don't want to love* you.

His thighs brushed the back of hers as he began spooning her. "Beth, you don't have to sleep alone tonight…"

She bolted upright and wiggled to the edge of the bed. But all her muddled brain could seem to wrap itself securely around was the mind-numbing, exquisite fact of sharing a bed with the one man in the world who could make her feel like a wanton. "Please tell me you're wearing something more decent to bed," she said, more like a plea. Why was he not odious? Why was he actually…likable? And sexy?

Sitting up, he glanced down at his mouthwatering chest and then frowned. "I don't feel like wearing anything." He met her gaze, then engulfed her shoulders in his hands and urged her closer. "Beth, I can feel how lonely you are, maybe that is why I want you. Will you understand what it's been like for me?"

She couldn't do this, open herself up like a present, then have his male expectations get a big bad whack of disappointment. She couldn't tear off the bandage, open the scars left by her past, no matter how sexy her husband. Hector had said she was frigid, and she feared, because he'd had a lover and had loved another woman, that he was probably right. "Landon, thank you…for helping me, but I don't think…"

He pulled a wad of his hair and groaned in frustration. "Bethany, I swear to God if you say thank you one more time…"

The dogs scratched the door.

"Aww, hell."

He stormed across to let the dogs inside and Beth heard them plop down on the carpet while Landon swiftly locked the door.

An excited, head-tingling sensation swept through her at the thought of being "trapped" with him.

Beth feigned sleep so Landon would stay on his side of the bed, and lying still in her pajamas while tucked in his sweet-smelling bed, she cursed herself for being ten times a fool when the mattress creaked and he slid in behind her. Of course nothing would stop this man from getting what he wanted. He grasped her waist and dragged her to him, and it took all her effort not to whimper.

She should have demanded another room, she knew, but there were guests in the house, and all would be occupied except one that belonged to his memories.

"Beth," he murmured, an erotic, decadent rasp in her eager little ear. He nibbled her earlobe, the full length of his granite-hard front pressing against her back. Her blood warmed like lava, melting her down to her bones. He was all flesh and muscle against her backside, except for those cotton trunks. Something hot and hard pressed between her buttocks, while his bare thighs grazed against hers as he slid his hand up her hip, under her shirt. She mewed softly.

A dog whined.

"Shut up, Mask." His hand slid up her abdomen, and Beth felt something unfurl inside her like a ribbon. Longing. Wanting. "Bethany," he roughly pleaded.

The sheet slid down her body as he slowly pried it down to her ankles. Beth had an urge to grab it back to her chest but then he'd know she was awake. She lay utterly still, felt his eyes caress her where his hand slid the T-shirt higher and higher. He cupped her buttock in his other hand, over her silken panties. She almost jolted when he groaned as though he were in terrible pain.

The dog whined again.

"Ah, hell." He left her, flung the door open. "Out, guys."

She heard them pad outside, then waited in anticipation, cold without the sheet and his body.

He came back to the bed and spooned her again,

tighter this time. He devoured her shoulder with his hungry mouth, again cupped her buttocks in his hand. "I can hear you breathe, Bethany. You're not asleep, you're nowhere even near asleep."

She fought to control her breathing but felt drunk with his scent, with the wanting spreading through her. This was such a bad idea…sleeping together… after days wondering and thinking about him and wanting to stay away….

He stroked the edge of her panties and tugged. "Can I take these off, hmm, can I take these off, Beth? I'll kiss you and touch you…that's all I'll do tonight, only what you want me to."

She closed her eyes tighter. His hunger made her feel so special, that she had to remind herself he had been in mourning, was known to be a solitary man, maybe felt lonely. He probably wanted to take something from Hector. It wasn't her he wanted—he just wanted sex.

But tonight's unexpected kiss came back vivid in her mind, and when he slid his hand to cup one aching breast, a sound escaped her.

"Ahaaaa—" he drew out the sound, lacing it with pleasure "—you want me?"

She made a sleepy sound, murmured, "Sooo tired," and rolled onto her stomach. He came with her, his mouth a moist flame ravaging her nape.

"It's been a long time for me, Beth. I won't pretend I don't want this. You."

He didn't stop touching her. He seemed to be memorizing her curves, seemed to have gone wild, like an animal, a caveman, as his hands traced her sides up and down, his hips rocking seductively against hers. "Turn around and kiss me again, Beth."

His body heat singed her back, and she could barely keep from moaning when he ground harder against her, tightening his hold on her hips, dragging his tongue up her neck. Her toes curled, and her sex rippled with wanting.

"Landon," she breathed. She forced herself to lay stiff as a board, but what he was doing felt entirely too good. She went lax, grabbed the pillow in front of her and moaned as he burrowed a hand under her body and pinched one nipple. "Oh." She arched back instinctively, and then nearly screamed in delight when he circled it with his thumb.

"Kiss me, Beth."

"I…" She turned around to face him, breathing hard. "I can't feel my tongue."

"God, you're so sexy all uninhibited like this, give it to me." Sweeping down, he closed his mouth over hers and gently suckled her tongue into his warm mouth. She felt that, goodness, she did. He tasted of champagne and her dizzied senses swam like frantic fishes in all kinds of directions as she let herself get even more drunk on her husband's intoxicating flavor.

She twisted her tongue around him and trailed her fingers over his chest before she remembered why this couldn't be. "Oh, no, we shouldn't—Landon, don't." Bolting upright and pushing him away, she smoothed her T-shirt with awkward, trembling hands. "I'm sorry. I can't. Not after the papers I signed."

He looked at her for a moment, then gave a long exhale. "I'm not losing another child. If you get pregnant, I want it."

Regret thickened her voice as she attempted to recover the sheets, needing something to clutch instead of the gorgeous man before her. "I'm not giving away a baby of mine, not even to you—I won't risk it. Excuse me but you're sitting on the sheets."

He cursed and drew her so close, embraced her so tight her breasts were crushed against his chest and her hands had to release the sheets she'd been trying to hang on to for sanity.

"Stop thinking so much and just feel for a minute," he growled, then smoothed his hands along her hair, and murmured, "It's all right, I'm not going to hurt you. I'm going to pleasure you, Bethany, I'm going to make you forget every man in your life but *me*."

Her insides disintegrated at that passionate vow. The need to kiss him, be with him, became so acute, she wanted to weep and scream in frustration. She wanted to say, *to hell with it!* and give her husband a wedding present no husband in his right mind ever forgets.

But he wasn't truly her husband, and she couldn't bear to repeat her mistakes, set herself up for heart-ache again. She'd been an innocent when she'd married Hector, but now she knew better.

She wiggled free of his hold and succeeded in pulling a part of the covers back over herself, as though they were the Berlin Wall itself—probably barely enough to keep a man like him away. Her voice, though she tried to keep it steady, broke in the end. "The black book is in the top nightstand drawer. I'm sure that's what you want to read to-night, being that you married me for it."

For a long, wretched minute, he didn't speak or breathe or move. Then her heart wept when he grabbed the book from the nightstand, carried it outside and shut the door behind him.

Nine

He'd gone through the headache thing with his first wife. Landon knew a willing woman when he saw one, and unfortunately, Bethany wasn't it.

Grim-faced behind his massive office desk, he waved the black book he was showing to his brothers. "The key to my success."

He handed it over, every single word he'd read in it seared into his mind.

Leaning back in his chair, he watched them sift through the pages, first Garrett with a thoughtful frown, then Julian John with raised eyebrows.

"One would think your disposition would change after last night," Garrett mulled out loud.

"I spent my wedding night reading that little gem there, not with my wife."

There was a bleak silence as Garrett digested this.

"Now why on earth would you do something so stupid?"

"She doesn't want me, Garrett."

"You're joking, right?"

"This is not something to joke about."

"She doesn't…desire you?" The words hung in the air, and they were so painful to hear, Landon found himself gritting his teeth. "I don't believe it."

"Believe it."

Julian glanced up from the book, raising both eyebrows. "Every woman wants you. You had girl-friends before you even had your first bike."

"Why wouldn't Beth want you?" Garrett demanded.

That was the worst question of them all. Landon remembered last night. How her nipples had pricked under his fingers. How her body had molded against his. He'd planned to give her no choice, make her beg for it.

He couldn't.

He didn't want her like this.

He wanted Beth willing—he wanted her to give him everything.

"Two names." He stuck out two fingers, pushing Beth from his thoughts. "Macy Jennings and Joseph Kennar. They're bought."

"No way."

"Yes way." He glared. "Apparently, Halifax sends them ten thousand dollar deposits every couple of months to ensure good press coverage on his 'miracle' treatments. We need to find a way to monitor their calls and hopefully get some solid evidence of their involvement. Plus it will help us determine what Hector is up to."

Garrett rolled up his shirt and made a note on the inside of his arm. "All right. Done. Can't wait to can those suckers when we're done with them."

"Right. And there's another interesting name near the last pages. You see it?" Landon pointed to the book Julian kept sifting through.

Julian's brown brow raised. "Miguel Gomez?"

Landon nodded affirmatively. "That same one. Miguel Gomez a.k.a. el Milagro. He's known for smuggling pharmaceuticals out of Mexico and to the States."

"Ahh, so the plot thickens…" Garrett said juicily, steepling his fingers. "The black book hath spoken."

"It has, indeed." Landon pulled out a sheaf of papers from the top folder of his stack and passed them to Garrett. "The insurance company's already halted some of Halifax's payments. There have been allegations of him duplicating claims, and they're thinking of suing."

Garrett skimmed. "Health care fraud. How fun. That shouldn't be too hard to prove."

"It shouldn't be." Landon's gaze shifted from one brother to the other while they both surveyed the info. "Now, if one of you gentlemen could arrange an interview with one of his assistants? The head nurse, maybe? We need her to talk, and we need her to talk dirty."

"I'm sure Jules will have them crying mercy in a minute."

With a cocksure smile, Julian dropped the book back on the desktop and folded his arms. "Of course."

Landon nodded. "Tomorrow would be good. Hell, today would be even better." He remembered his wife's frustration over not seeing her son, and fresh determination surged through him. "I'm meeting with our lawyer at two, I need to fill him in on this development. Halifax's been keeping the child away from her, and Beth's anxious to see him. We need to move fast. I want to prove the good doctor isn't fit company for an ape, much less a little boy. It would be easy to accomplish if we get the nurse to testify against him—as a character witness."

"Consider it done," Julian said with the assurance all Gages were known for.

"Halifax wants Beth back, Landon, you know he does."

The quiet words struck a chord, and for a moment, Landon felt them reverberate in his body.

Frowning at the thought of her ever even considering to so much as talk to Halifax, he gazed at today's headlines scattered over his desk.

Surprise Wedding!

Millionaire Magnate Back at the Altar.

Love in the Era of Money.

He was pleased there wasn't hostility in any of the articles—crucial for her to get David back. But then there was that other article that irked Landon beyond normal. It contained the picture of one sick man ominously holding up his forefinger.

Halifax: "It's not over 'til it's over!"

"Did Garrett tell you Mom invited your wife to the range today?"

Surprised, he glanced up at his youngest brother. Julian rarely kidded around. "To the shooting range? Mom?"

"Yep. And Beth."

Landon couldn't help it. He threw his head back and laughed. The image of Beth, bloodthirsty and hungover, holding a rifle in those sweet little hands. Damn, it was funny. "Right. Well, then." He shook his head in disbelief and then flicked on his monitor, determined to get to work.

"Figured out how to romance your wife yet?" Garrett asked.

Landon busily scribbled a thought on a legal pad before him. *Help her find something to do from home. Buy her cranberries.* "Focusing on Halifax now."

A snort from his brother. "Nothing stirs a woman's libido like talking about an ex."

Landon ignored the bait and waved them off. "Whatever. Just get out of here."

He had things to do.

A business to run, a man to destroy, a child to recover and a woman to woo....

"See my dear? Now, after holding a gun and firing that haystack clean off the line, don't you realize we can do anything?"

Two weeks later, Beth found herself in the shooting range again.

Squinting her eyes under the glowing sun as a shock of adrenaline rushed through her veins, she lowered her rifle and drew in a calming breath. She'd started to adore her mother-in-law and their weekly visits to the shooting range. "Well, I didn't quite hit it just yet, Eleanor."

"Oh, but twenty or thirty more tries, we both know that haystack is dead."

Within three seconds, Eleanor aimed her rifle, shot and reloaded.

"Landon's my eldest."

She shot and reloaded.

"He's been alone too long."

She shot and reloaded.

"I hope that doesn't impair his ability to interact with a woman."

She shot. Then lowered her rifle to give Beth a turn.

Beth aimed, lips pursed with effort, her hands weighed by the long, sleek weapon. "He's very nice, Mrs. Gage."

"Nice." She humphed. "I don't think he'd like to be called that by you."

"Well, we're not staying married forever," Beth said, peering through the hole as she sighted one fat haystack. "This was a mutual understanding. Spurred by our mutual hate for the same man."

"Yes yes yes. But I saw the way my son looked at you. And I saw no hate in those eyes." Even through a set of thick goggles, Beth felt Eleanor's dark eyes scrutinize her profile, as though all the answers to the woman's questions were written on Beth's cheek. "And when you look at him, I see no hate in yours, either. Nor indifference, for that matter. I'm an old goat, and I know a couple of things when I see them."

Beth blushed, gritted her teeth and pressed her finger into the trigger. Pop! The bullet flew—Lord knows where it landed. It did not hit a single target.

"Your mother and I chatted yesterday." Eleanor winked at Beth before she aimed once more, rendered positively feral by those goggles and with that secretive smile she wore. "We're playing canasta today. And…other games. Games like matchmaking my son with her daughter. Isn't that fun?"

Beth's eyebrows furrowed as she watched the woman take a perfect shot. Bam! "If your matchmaking is as good as your shooting," Beth grumbled, "then no, it's not going to be fun at all."

This would not do.

Matchmaking among mothers, the last thing Beth needed at this point. Specifically, because her husband seemed to be the sexiest thing walking the planet. And because apparently Beth wasn't as frigid as her ex-husband had led her to believe.

The frustration of waiting for a hearing had been riding on her nerves. Every day when Landon arrived from work Beth asked the same question over dinner: Do we have a hearing yet?

I'm on it, he'd say.

She was beginning to wonder if they would ever reach that day. And in the meantime she was suffering, totally, wretchedly suffering. True, Kate's website launch so far had been a moderate success. A few inquiries in the form of emails had already trickled in, and on a burst of inspiration, Kate and Beth had decided to add a "Share your Recipe" section to the website. But even those fun plans and little satisfactions failed to quell the internal turmoil in her.

Landon Gage had her sleeping in her bed alone at night for the past two weeks imagining things like sliding into his bed and smoothing her hands up his chest and into his hair and...

Shaking off the thoughts, Beth stormed into his room when she heard him come into the house. "Landon, our mothers are playing canasta."

"And?"

Her heart tripped—in a white buttoned shirt, without a belt and in his black slacks, Landon looked rumpled, ruffled, gorgeous. "And...and, and I think they're conspiring against us."

"In what sense?"

Bethany watched wide-eyed as he began to unbutton his shirt, then couldn't remember what she planned to say. When she did, she realized she sounded ridiculous. As if there was the remote possibility that either of them would fall, which there wasn't. No matter how much matchmaking. Was there? "Oh, forget it. How was your day?"

"Tiring." And in that instant, a thought teased her: *What if he were really my husband? What if he'd come home from work and David would jump on him like his dogs did and he'd smile and rumple his hair...*

Landon produced something from his pockets. "Here. I brought you something."

She stared in interest down at a book. It was a cookbook, and even better, it was one she'd never read before. Her chest squeezed as she stroked her fingers along the glossy surface. It was such a nice gesture on his part. A gesture which told her he didn't mind finding his kitchen in a mess while she explored new recipes. And which told her, in a way, that at least a couple of minutes today, he'd thought about her, too. "Thank you, I don't know what to say. Thanks from me and…thanks from Catering, Canapés and Curry."

"Nice name. I'm guessing you came up with it since Kate had failed to find one for over a year?"

She nodded, still so touched she felt stroked all over.

Landon crossed the room toward her, and Beth

nervously licked her lips when he raised one bronzed big hand to cup her cheek. His thumb, gentle and warm, wiped a smudge of dirt off the tip of her nose. "You went shooting today?"

That touch alone felt like an electric current that started in her nose and ended with a jolt in Beth's toes. "Y-yes. I love it. I always feel so…powerful."

Her cheeks flamed as he disappeared into his bathroom, turned on the shower, then came back out and pulled his unbuttoned shirt out of his pants. Her gaze felt glued to his, she couldn't seem to pull free of his quiet stare.

"Your mother insinuated that my mom and she think…They're trying to get us together. They're crazy. A marriage based on nothing but common hatred," she said.

He nodded indulgently, all bronzed skin and gleaming muscles as he shrugged off the garment, and his hands went to his pants. Beth watched, wide-eyed, as he began to unzip. Her breasts tingled. A prick of awareness danced across her skin.

"What else do we have in common other than Hector, I mean…" She trailed off when he stripped to his underwear. Her lungs closed off all air.

He stood before her for a moment, as sexy and comfortable in his skin as an underwear model, while a prominent bulge pushed against the stark white cotton of his trunks. Even down there, Landon Gage was bigger than Hector.

He was more man, more everything.

In other words, too much for Beth.

She became aware of how fast her chest heaved when he gave her a sardonic smile. "Are you staying here and watching or are you letting me take a bath?"

Beth stumbled back a step, a trembling hand reaching for the doorknob. "I'm leaving."

"Close the door, Beth."

She turned to go, but then spun around. "Landon…"

He kicked off his trunks, his back to her, and when she saw his nakedness all of her blood seemed to rush to the center of her being, where it gathered into a burning pool of desire. Her breath left her completely, and the book slid from her fingers and landed with a thud on the floor.

Landon's buttocks were so muscled, they clenched as he stepped out of his underwear—every small and large muscle of his body taut and rock-like under his skin. He glanced past his shoulder. "Yeah?"

She shook her head to clear her thoughts. But oh. *Oooh.* She'd been wondering for days, had been aching for a peek of him, she was so bad, and suddenly this was so embarrassing.

"I'm no good at this. Landon, I…" She clung to the door handle behind her, her knuckles white as she squeezed it for support. "I'm sorry about our wedding night. My life was shattered when I left him," she hurriedly whispered, "and I know that I will be leaving you and I really want to…be prepared, you know? I guess I just worry if I make others believe it, a part of me will believe it, too, and I don't want to, it's not *real.* Nothing's real to me but David."

He reached into the bathroom for a towel, and wrapped it easily around his narrow hips. "But we expect nothing." Even half covered she could hardly think. His chest was so beautiful, all of him making her mouth water, especially the smoldering proposal in his eyes. "I don't expect anything from you, Beth, nor you from me, except to trample Hector. Neither of us is hoping the other will love us like we love or be with us forever."

"But our mothers hope."

He started forward. "Mothers will always hope."

He caught her shoulders and she squeaked and flattened back against the door. "No, please no, no kissing!"

He let his arms drop at his sides and cursed low in his throat as he squeezed his eyes shut. "Fine."

He stepped away, jaw clenched taut. "Fine. If you change your mind, you let me know."

"Landon, are you angry?"

He didn't answer.

"Landon!"

"I'm not angry, Beth, just get out of my room." He grabbed the cookbook and shoved it into her chest before he stalked away.

"Wait…" she called him, and he turned at the bathroom door. Their gazes locked.

He was dark and tall and looking very much a husband, while she stood there by the opposite door, with a new dress she'd bought on sale that he hadn't even noticed, a huge knot in her stomach and a horrible sense of loss. She clutched the book to her chest. "It's not you, it's me."

"No," he said, tersely. "It's him."

He closed the bathroom door, and for a minute, Beth stood there frozen and confused. Then she charged into her room, tossed herself on the bed and buried her face under the pillow. She screamed into the down, a scream of total and wretched frustration.

What had he meant by that? If Landon thought this had anything to do with Hector, he was *wrong*.

It was David who worried her, David who kept her locked in her room at night, David and how he deserved a stable future, not living through another heartbreaking divorce.

She clenched her eyes shut and tried to shut down the images that tormented her.

Landon in the shower. *Naked.* Landon naked with all that thick muscle. Landon giving her a mere book and making her feel like he'd given her a piece of the moon.

She groaned. She went under, yanked the covers up to her head and tried not to think of his hot kisses, his surprising smiles, his penetrating stares.

Impossible. Vivid, mushy and sweaty thoughts of her husband made her hot, and squirmy, and it made her ashamed.

She couldn't do this. Sure, she could do *this*— pretend marriage. But she couldn't do the rest.

Her and Landon's relationship was just a convenient business arrangement that would open beautiful possibilities for her future—her son, specifically.

But even as she reminded herself to keep Landon's and her expectations in line, in her mind she pictured being coiled so tightly around Landon neither of them could breathe.

Beth! she chastised herself. *Remember what happens when they want what you can't give. What happens when you let yourself fall in love with a man who doesn't really want or need you.*

Sighing, she rolled to her side, and an ache settled around her chest as she thought of David. She closed her eyes and imagined him sleeping, always cherubic—like her very own angel. And she prayed he dreamt of gumdrops and licorice sticks, of puppies and kittens, of anything but the hell going on between his mother and father. "Good night, David. Sleep tight."

Beth knew for sure that she would not.

Because just down the hall in his big room, in his big shower, bare-chested and most definitely alone, was Landon.

Ten

The weeks passed, each day loaded with a strange mix of companionship and charged pauses, growing friendship and stolen touches, talk of revenge and looks that were heated with longing.

This morning Beth had a strange hole inside her. She couldn't take his kindness any longer—it made her feel weak and hopeful and besotted, when all she wanted was to feel angry and abused again and concentrate on what most mattered to her.

"Where are we going?" she asked, tearing her eyes away from the scenery and meeting his sharp silver gaze.

Landon lounged in the backseat of the Navigator this Saturday morning, carefree and relaxed in tan slacks and a white polo, but his gaze shone with interesting secrets. One corner of his lips kicked up a notch. "I've arranged for you to see David."

Beth's every muscle jerked at that, and her heart went bonkers in her chest. "You have? How? When?"

"I spoke to a mother of one of his school friends. He's over for a play date today and I thought—"

"You did not!" she gasped, then covered her mouth with trembling hands. *"Ohmigod!"*

"Breathe, Beth," he said, leaning forward in his seat, his eyes crinkling at the sides. "It's a bit risky. We're violating the custody arrangement, but we're compensating your friend with a generous amount in exchange for her silence—and nobody will know as long as David understands he needs to keep quiet. Do you think we can pull this off?"

Her chest moved. "Yes, God, yes! David and I have been keeping secrets from his father for forever—he'll never tell!"

It depressed her to think that David was too old for his years, but it was true. Ever since he was three, he'd seemed to notice how easily his father angered. He'd loathed the fact that every time his dad felt displeased he'd issue a silent treatment that made both David and Beth want to hide.

But how had Landon managed to set this up? Her mind whizzed with questions, but they all ended with one simple fact, one unerring truth: no matter why, or where, or how Landon had managed to schedule a meeting with her son, the only important thing was that he *had.*

She would see her son today.

She felt so big all of a sudden it was a wonder she fit inside the car.

As they rounded a corner, Beth's attention became riveted on a familiar redbrick house. The fenced front lawn was green and trimmed, and a set of bicycles were tossed over on their sides in the driveway. She spotted two kids playing by the rosebushes and her heart soared at the sight of the blond little boy—*her* little boy. She almost heard music in the background, could practically see his aura shine like an angel's.

Barely a second after the car halted, Beth shoved the door open and ran across the asphalt to the fence. "David!" she shouted, as she entered the yard and closed the gate be-hind her.

He pivoted instantly, a baseball in his hand. "Mom?"

His fingers tightened around the ball, but he didn't run to her. He stayed frozen in place, in loose jeans and a striped T-shirt. He eyed his good friend Jonas first, as if asking for his permission, but all Jonas did was stick his hand out for the ball.

"Sweetie, oh, darling baby," Beth choked as she dropped to her knees and stretched out her arms. "I've missed you so much."

He crashed into her and Beth's eyes welled up as they clutched each other. He smelled of shampoo and grass and little boy, and for a moment Beth inhaled as much as she could.

When her pulse calmed, she began asking him what he'd been doing, reminded him his father could not know about this if they wanted to be together again, and then she remembered Landon, now leaning against the car, and she seized David's little hand and rose to face her husband. The sun made his dark hair gleam and glazed his tanned skin like warmed honey.

His expression was inscrutable, but there was emotion in his eyes. The silver in them had intensified to a sharp polished metal.

She brought David over to the fence. "Landon, this is my son, David. David, this is Mr. Gage."

Landon's son would be his age, she realized. Had he wanted to be a dad? He seemed to be ruthlessly suppressing the urge to go back into the car.

"Is he my new daddy?" David asked, blinking.

Her motherly instinct didn't take long to kick in. Beth quickly began to arrange his shirt, comb his hair, and out of habit, checked his temperature.

"He's mommy's special friend, my love. And he's doing everything he can to bring you home with us. With me. Do you want that?"

"Yeah," he admitted.

Both man and boy continued regarding each other warily. Landon with a hand in his pocket, the other restless at his side.

David kicked the grass. "Does he like horses?"

Smiling because that's just the thing that her David, the animal lover, would say, she hugged him again. Tight. Had he grown? He'd grown an inch, she was sure of it! "He has two big dogs," she told him excitedly. "They're as big as lions. You would like them."

"Jonas's mother said you would come. I didn't believe her but I wanted you to. She said I could make you something and I made you this." From the back pocket of his jeans, he retrieved a paper and gradually unfolded it to show her a drawing of spaceships and stars that read, "David+Mom."

"Oh, my! Well, there, Commander, that is one dangerous aircraft, and is that big heart mine?"

He nodded, his grin already showing a missing tooth. Beth thought of how they would play astronauts and cowboys and anything else they could conjure when they got back together. She'd deepen her voice to sound like the villain so David could trap her and be the hero.

She rumpled his hair and stole a peek back at the house to find Mary Wilson standing by the kitchen window with little Jonas now at her side, watching their reunion with a smile.

Beth nodded at her and mouthed, "Thank you."

As though having at last convinced his legs to move, Landon approached the fence, still so quiet. He reached over the top of the pickets. "Hi, David." He offered his knuckled fist, as Beth supposed he might do with his brothers, and said, "If you bump it, it means we're friends."

David frowned, not easily sold. "Can I see your dogs?"

Landon didn't seem to know what to say. He kept staring down at her son with a mixture of confusion and pain.

Beth blurted, "You can ride them like ponies if you'd like to!"

That did it. Her son's entire face changed from wariness to full adoration. "Okay."

And he lifted his balled little hand and bumped it against Landon's big one.

"Thank you."

Minutes after leaving David, Beth's excitement

had dimmed and morphed into a fuzzy, warm flutter as Thomas drove them home. She felt like hugging Landon but instead fidgeted with the pearl button on the lapel of her shirt. David's drawing was neatly stashed inside her purse. David's scent, his smiles, every word he'd said, had been tucked away inside her, too. Her heart threatened to burst.

"He seemed happy to see you," Landon said, his eyes glimmering with pride.

"Yes." Beth felt her chest contract, remembering how David's face had lit like a sunbeam when she'd told him they'd be together soon. When? he'd asked, again and again. When…

A lump gathered in her throat. Even after such a wonderful day, tonight there would still be an injustice in the fact that someone else would be tucking her son into bed.

Beth realized with a start that Landon's thigh and her own pressed together, that they were sitting too close, and that it would be rude to slide away. So she tried not to notice how thick his thigh was. How hard.

She felt she needed to say something but didn't know where to begin, or how to organize her thoughts. Her armor had been stripped away; she trembled with emotion, excitement and something else. He smelled so good up close, like the wind. Like a man.

Landon gazed out the window. He looked terribly big and terribly lonely. All her walls against him, all her reservations, seemed to have morphed fully into all these awed and inspired feelings of admiration and respect and desire. God, what was she supposed to do with these?

"Your son…" she began.

"Nathan," he corrected.

"Nathan. He'd be around David's age?"

He nodded.

Should she have brought up this subject? It seemed to be the one on his mind, but speaking of the boy without telling Landon what she knew proved difficult. "This must've been hard for you."

He signaled at her, and let his eyes sweep meaningfully over her. "Not particularly. You seem very happy, Bethany."

Her cheeks heated up, and she averted her face. "It's not easy being a parent. You never imagine you could care so much."

He made a sound, like a snort. "And yet the instant you hear that wail and stare into their eyes, they've got you."

"They do!" she agreed.

They shared smiles, and the comfortable quiet

between them morphed into something smoldering and sensual.

"You know," Landon said, so softly she felt the whisper in the interior of the car like a tangible caress. "I still don't know when you got me, Beth." He cocked his head and regarded her with the eyes of a man who knew too much. "Maybe when you came spitting fire—asking for my help. Or maybe when I see you looking at me the way you do."

Flooded with mortification, Beth raised a halting hand and lowered her face. "Landon, don't."

He reached out and cupped her shoulder, grazing her arm with his thumb. "Don't what?"

The heat radiating from his body made her squirm. The ache inside her continued opening, like a ravenous animal, turning her desire into pain. "Don't talk to me like this." *Yes, please do, tell me if you care, too.*

No, he mustn't!

He leaned back negligently and studied her with impressive calm. The sunlight streaming through the window cast playful shadows on his profile. "But you like it when I talk to you like this."

She struggled against a barrage of emotion. She did like it, she loved it, but she shook her head fast, still not ready to admit anything.

Landon Gage wasn't a pillar she could lean on

tomorrow, wouldn't be a steady presence in her life. There were just these few…moments. With him. Dangerous moments, crowded with dangerous thoughts.

"I don't…want to."

"Now you're blushing."

"Because you're flirting."

"Flirting." A sprinkle of laughter danced across his eyes. "I'm being honest with my wife."

She raised her eyes to his. "Then can you honestly tell me you're not trying to seduce me?"

He offered no argument for a moment, but then said, in a voice that broached no argument, "If I were trying to seduce you, you'd be right here." Meaningfully, he patted his lap, and her eyes hurt at the image of the prominent bulge between his parted thighs. "You'd be right here, right now. And I wouldn't be sleeping alone tonight—nor would you."

She tried reining in her jumbled thoughts, but couldn't seem to get past the words "seduce" and "you'd be right here." "Then you're just playing some sort of game?" Her voice came out unsteady.

He shook his head. "I'm definitely not playing."

"Then what?" she persisted. "What's this about? What is it that you want from me?"

"You really want to know what I want?"

"I want to know what you want, yes!"

"Your trust, Beth. Before you give me anything else, I want your *trust*."

They engaged in a brief staring contest, Landon's eyes scalding, Beth struggling to tame the wild impulse to put her lips on his beautiful stern ones.

Stricken by the realization that Landon always brought out the lonely, impulsive teenager in her, she lost the staring contest and glanced down at her purse on her lap. "What makes you think I don't trust you?"

"Do you?"

She opened her mouth to say yes, yes, she did, despite not wanting to, when Thomas interrupted. "Sir, I've got orders to drive you to the office right away."

"First we drop off Bethany."

Beth frowned, inched a bit farther away, hoping distance between them would give her distance from emotions, too. "Something important at the office?"

"Not really." He shifted in his seat, his legs opening wider now that he had more space.

"If you'd pardon me, sir." Thomas cleared his throat and caught her gaze in the rearview mirror. "It's Mr. Gage's birthday today, Mrs. Gage. The office always celebrates despite his say in the matter."

Beth gaped in stunned surprise. "It's your birthday."

His birthday. Her husband's birthday.

Oh, wow. She must be the worst wife in the history of the world.

She hadn't known…

She hadn't known about his birthday.

But she tried to reassure herself, telling herself, in her mind, that she knew Landon in ways others didn't.

She knew that his loyalty was steadfast and not easily given, knew that he'd done right by his first wife and generally right by everyone around him. She knew that he was quiet and thoughtful but knew how to laugh, and that his smiles—unlike Hector's—were real and reached his eyes.

Pursing her lips in determination, she opened the window. "Thomas, I'll be accompanying my husband."

Landon didn't protest.

He glanced out at the cityscape as though it didn't matter, but his fingers began to drum over his thigh.

Ten minutes later, when they arrived at the top floor of the *San Antonio Daily*, the noise was deafening. Eighty people circulated in the office space, if not more. Balloons had been hung from the ceiling. Computer screens held birthday greetings and songs were blaring from speakers. People wore funny hats.

It warmed Beth to witness this, to know that Landon was so respected his people would do this for him. It made her proud to walk next to him.

"Goodness, your people love you," she exclaimed, wide-eyed.

He cocked one sleek eyebrow. "Surprised?"

"Amazed," she admitted, and impulsively reached up to smooth back a strand of dark hair that had fallen on his forehead. "But not in the least bit surprised."

This seemed to please him, and his grip tightened on her elbow as he guided her across the hall.

Of course, his brothers were present, too. Situated right in the center of it all. Julian John uncorked the champagne, pouring the liquid into dozens of glasses, then took a swig directly from the bottle and kept it to himself. Clad all in black, which suited his dark good looks, Garrett was fighting with Kate over who got to wear the silly hat she kept planting over his head. Beth doubted Kate was catering, but she was there because she was practically family to the Gages, had grown up in their household when her father, the Gages' bodyguard, had been killed in the line of duty.

Landon greeted everyone by name and introduced Beth as his wife, and he put his arm around her. Beth felt shy and self-conscious, but when the partygoers returned to their mingling and Landon focused on her, holding her lightly against him, all her awkwardness melted under a creamy swirl of excitement.

"This is a really nice party," she whispered, touching his arm briefly as she said this.

The candidness in Landon's gaze affected her almost as much as the whisper of his fingertip trailing along her jaw. "It's even nicer with you in it."

A shiver raced through her, impossible to suppress.

God, what was happening between them?

Neither seemed to stop touching each other, neither seemed to stop staring, to want to put distance between them or be anywhere else but near.

Before she made a fool of herself, Beth told her husband the sweets buffet called to her and managed a smooth escape, leaving Landon with his mother.

"Never seen him smile like today," an older woman hovering by the candy, who'd been introduced as Julian's assistant, told Beth. "Mr. Landon,

I mean. And all the girls and I agree it's because of *you*."

Landon smiling…

Because of *her?*

The thought moved her so powerfully Beth couldn't speak through the ball of emotion in her throat. Because Landon Gage not only made her happy sometimes, too, but he also made her ache. Ache for him. For more.

She picked through the sweets and popped a handful of dried cranberries into her mouth, but they did little to appease the building urge to scan the room and find him.

She wanted him.

Admired him.

Loved his attitude, his strength, his dynamism. Loved his eyes, his face, even the way he scowled. She loved his… She loved all of him.

Oh, God, love, she thought with a wrenching in her stomach.

She loathed to think that *this* was how it felt—the helpless, excited, burning and frightened sensation she got every time she saw and thought about and stood near Landon.

"Blow it, brother!" Garrett cheered as they surrounded him near the three-tiered cake and the pair of flaming candles that boasted the big blue number 33.

Chuckling softly while shaking his head, Landon positioned himself at the end of the long table. That flattering white polo shirt really suited him, Beth thought dreamily from afar. He had such a thick, bronzed neck, his shoulders so hard—

"Beth!" Kate called her. "Get over there next to Lan for a picture. He won't bite you." She stuck her tongue out and held up the camera. "Not that I can say the same for the cake."

Landon trapped her gaze from across the room. Was it caring she saw in his incredible eyes?

Weak-kneed, Beth started walking over, her heart pounding like a drum. At that very moment, Kate's guarantee of him not biting didn't reassure her. A gleam of possessiveness glimmered in Landon's eyes, and the mine-mine-mine! they seemed to echo set the tips of her breasts on fire where they pressed against her top.

He watched her advance. The way his attention homed in on her made her blood simmer. If they'd been anywhere else, anywhere else but in a roomful of people, Beth didn't know what they'd be doing. No, that was a lie. She had a pretty good idea of what they'd be doing, what they could be doing— like regular husbands and wives.

"Come on, brother, make a wish!"

Landon bent forward, and as his eyes met Beth's over the candles, a slow smile spread on his lips and made her thighs turn liquid. Desire wound around her like a vine, bringing with it a world of emotions she couldn't suppress. Love…

They weren't normal husband and wife, but they were more than Beth had ever been with her ex-husband. More connected than Beth had ever imagined feeling to another living thing. The candles smoked as he blew them out all at once. Crazily, she wondered what on earth a man who had everything could wish for. And it struck her.

He wished for me.

The thought was irresistible. Her hands clenched at her sides, and she could almost hear the last weak little barrier inside her crumpling.

And maybe all my life I've been wishing for him.

Something accompanied them home.

Something searing and undeniable. Electricity leapt from him to her, her to him, charging Beth's nerve endings as they entered the quiet house.

They took the stairs side by side.

Expectation tickled inside of her as she reached her bedroom door.

She half hoped Landon would draw up behind

her, half expected for him to turn her around and claim a heated kiss.

He didn't.

Startled when he said good-night, Beth heard his footsteps, muffled on the carpet as he made his way down the hall.

With an awful disappointment, she slipped into her spacious lonely bedroom, then surveyed the contents of her closet.

She had to do something, wouldn't forgive herself if his kind actions went unrewarded, if her wanting continued to be unappeased. She wasn't sure where this determination, this courage or this desperate want had come from; she only knew she needed her husband. She needed to show him her loyalties were with him, her gratitude, her respect and desire. Her trust.

Were with him.

Dragging in a breath, she eased into a little number she'd never worn before, and then without thinking about it too much, quietly made her way to Landon's bedroom.

The door stood partway open.

Her blood rushed so fast and heady in her veins it deafened her to the single word she spoke. "Landon."

His head shot up at the sound of his name.

They stared in the quiet, sizing each other up.

Beth in the threshold to his bedroom, Landon in bed with the covers to his waist, bare-chested and bronzed, already with a book in his hands.

Her eyes hurt, he was so compelling. Hard, bulging muscles stretched taut across his broad shoulders. She could see his biceps and the defined bands of his abs before they disappeared under the crisp white sheets.

Nervously, she wet her lips and forced herself to shut the door behind her. "Did you have a nice birthday?"

Clenching his jaw, Landon set his reading material aside. "Thank you, yes. Did you need anything?"

His clipped tone hinted that he wanted her to go, and for three long heartbeats, Beth considered it.

But she remained, struggling for the words. *Love me.*

Landon waited in silence, then let out a sigh. "Bethany, I'm hanging by a thread in more ways than you can imagine. If it's nothing urgent, I suggest you go back to your room now."

She did not know what to say. She'd been so insistent they keep a healthy distance, she now realized it would be a struggle to let him know that things… had changed. Everything. Had changed.

Breathing deeply, she brought her hand to the tie

of her silk robe around her neck and fiddled with it. "I'd like to sleep here," she said.

Frowning, Landon sat up, looking all gorgeous and puzzled and frustrated. "Is there something wrong with your bed?"

Don't say no, please don't send me away.

She'd never seduced a man, and the thought of being rejected made her cheeks heat up and her legs want to aim in another direction.

"It's empty."

With a low groan, he banged the back of his head against the headrest and closed his eyes. "Ah, Beth. How can I say this…" His Adam's apple bobbed as he swallowed.

"Please don't turn me away."

A tremor spread through her as she waited, clenching the fabric from her nightgown in her hands.

If he denied her, she'd be devastated. Devastated.

Landon cursed under his breath and rolled to the other side of the bed. "Let me put on something, all right? And we can talk."

Mute, Beth gaped at his gorgeous body as he eased out of bed, the ripple of muscle down his back as he plunged into his pajama bottoms. She gazed longingly at the covers, wanted to slip inside them, where Landon had been naked just now. His sheets would be warm, but she didn't know if they were welcoming.

"What is it, exactly, that you want from me," he growled as he strode over wearing loose cotton sleep pants, haphazardly tied.

She bit her lower lip in uncertainty. "Kiss me good-night?" That was as close as she got to asking him to take her, and apparently he didn't believe his ears.

He stared in wonder, his expression revealing he still didn't seem to know what to make of this visit.

"Not like a friend or a partner—like a husband," she amended.

Understanding made his eyes flash.

He clenched his jaw so tight, a muscle jumped in the back, then he plunged both his hands into her hair and set his forehead on hers. "Do you want to be kissed by your husband?" he hissed.

"Yes." She linked her hands behind his head and shuddered in expectation. "Please."

He shut his eyes, let go a breath, and didn't do anything for a long, long time.

Rolling his head against hers, he made a low, hungry sound. "Now tell me," he said slowly, roughly, his voice ragged with desire, "you want your husband to make love to you, too."

* * *

She didn't answer for what felt like a year.

It was a dream, it had to be, but Beth felt too slim and warm to be a figment of his imagination. Landon had a desperate urge to get close to her. Closer. To feel her body around his, penetrate its depths, fill them with his essence.

He'd never gone without sex so long, but now it wasn't sex he craved, it was mating with his wife, finding that union, that closeness. Searching her, finding her secrets, delving into the darkest parts of her, allowing her access to his.

He didn't know what would happen if he kissed her. He didn't know if he could *stop.*

She'd asked for a kiss, but Landon wanted her to want more, want it all.

He bent his head when she didn't respond and watched her reaction as he grazed her lips.

She trembled against him. "Landon," she moaned weakly and the way she uttered his name catapulted his need to alarming levels.

His heart pounded. *Stop stop stop, you idiot, you're losing control.*

But she wanted him. She was here, she was asking for it.

"Do you, Beth?"

An anticipatory groan rumbled up from his chest

as he whisked her lips again, holding his breath at the tantalizing contact. "Do you want me… Landon…to make love to you?"

He moved his lips over hers, gently attempting to coax them apart. Her hands tightened at his nape as he slid his hands up her back and held her against him. He gave himself a minute to savor the right-ness of her body against his, the difference in their forms, and deepened the contact when she opened a little.

"I won't stop," he rasped, seizing her plush bottom lip between both of his. "I'm going to touch you, and lick you, and strip you down to your skin, and I won't stop until morning."

When she shifted in his arms just slightly, giving him the impression she wanted him even closer, he lost control and slid out his tongue to taste. Once. Side to side, his tongue traced the entry of her lips. "Say it," he whispered. "Say the words to me."

"Yes," she breathed.

His tenuous hold on his control threatened to snap when her lips parted, and her warm, damp tongue curled seductively around his. The coy caress de-stroyed him. Patience, measure, reason fled. Need flared in his body like a rising tide of lava, and a hunger pent up for years surfaced with a vengeance. He crushed her to him and opened his mouth wide, kissing her like only a man too starved or too desperate could. His initial sampling became a feast. A claiming. His claiming.

He growled when her lips moved with the same frantic eagerness as his, and still he demanded more. He drank of her, letting the sweetness and the honey and the taste of her flood his mouth in a flavor so intoxicating it made his head spin. He'd underestimated the power of her. The temptress in disguise with the worried eyes and the heart of a lion that had driven him insane for weeks.

She moaned into his mouth, and desire ricocheted within the walls of his body, painful in its force. The prenup, the fake wedding, it all vanished from his thoughts. He could only think of his bed. With this woman in it.

He tore his mouth free and slipped his hands around to cup her tight, round bottom, then dragged her flat against him, letting her feel the painful length of his erection straining against the fabric.

He gazed into her surprised eyes, curling his hands to get a handful of soft, willing flesh as he covered her mouth again. They moaned in unison.

He opened his lips over hers, drinking what she gave him, demanding more. He'd thought she was a vision. He'd thought she was a dream. And he couldn't stop kissing her, touching her, thrusting his tongue inside her depths to taste her. Hot. So hot. So sweet.

He added teeth to the kiss, biting, nibbling at her, and when she tightened her arms around his neck, he thought his chest would implode.

"Landon," she said in a reverent whisper as her mouth trailed down his chest, quick and hungry. No, voracious. Landon felt dizzy as she peppered warm, moist kisses on his heated flesh and stroked her fingers down the muscles of his abdomen.

Yes, he thought as the blood stormed through his body, *yes yes* yes.

His every muscle taut with need, he guided her back and urged her down on the bed. She fell there, her skin luminous in the moonlight, every shadow dancing over her body making it clear her night-gown was sheer.

His erection pushed even harder, ready to rip through his pants. "Did you come to my room to seduce me?" He trembled knowing the answer, and leaned over her waiting female body, watching her nod slowly, almost hesitantly.

"Yes."

She came up to her knees and reached out for his drawstring. But Landon planted a hand on her tummy and forced her onto her back again, in lust, in agony. "Ladies first." He couldn't understand his

own words. His breathing had morphed into something haggard.

With slow, barely steady hands, he tugged the
ends of the ribbons that held her nightgown together.
One by one the bows came undone.

"Show me what's mine," he said, softly.

Her eyes darkened with hunger as she raised her
shaky hands to her throat, keeping the garment
closed. Then the fabric slid down one shoulder, then
lower, exposing the round globes of her breasts, her
flat stomach, and then…

He swallowed the aching lump in his throat. "Put
it aside," he said gruffly.

Every rustle of fabric was audible through the
silence—until every inch of her was revealed to
him.

His body throbbed painfully but he hesitated
before lying over her, unsure of what his hands
would do, knowing how he could lose his mind
touching her. She had gotten to him. He had wanted
her the first day when she came to ask for help,
had wanted her every night when he woke up in a
wrenching, unfulfilled sweat produced by dreams
so vivid and erotic he would remember them even
by day. He'd been fantasizing about a family with
her, a real family.

He would never let her go.

He grabbed her wrists gently between his hands and guided her arms up over her head, pinning her there, so he could see her in the dim lighting.

She gazed up at him, her eyes shining with need and want.

Holding her wrists trapped in one hand, he slid the other between her heaving breasts, past her navel, to caress the silky curls at the apex of her thighs. "Been waiting to touch you." He stroked the glistening folds with one finger, then inserted it into her tight sheath and she gasped and arched back in pleasure. "I need to see, Beth…your face…hear the sounds you make."

Her eyes drifted shut as he inserted a second finger, her face twisting into a grimace of pleasure. "Please," she said, and tears laced her voice. "Touch me."

"Where? Where, Beth baby? Here?" Releasing her wrists, he cupped one breast and roughly scraped his thumb across the pebbled nipple, pleased when she vaulted up to his hand.

Her voice shook. "Everywhere."

She looked so damned beautiful, still shy somehow. And beautiful.

His heart beat so hard he thought he'd crack a rib, and inside of him, a painful need began to squeeze his gut. Two wives. One had betrayed him to Halifax. And this one…his little Buffy. He couldn't even think of her betraying him, couldn't fathom how it would feel.

"Beth," he huskily prodded, seizing her hand and guiding it under the elastic of his pants. "That's for you." He twirled his tongue across the tip of one breast, breathing hard as she enveloped his erection. He pitched his hips deeper into her palm. "To pleasure you." Growling, he turned his head to lick the other breast, suckling it into his mouth. "To show you how much I want you."

"I want you, too. I want you so much, Landon."

The words, what he craved and so much more when she combined it with a flutter of her fingers against the length of his aching hardness, undid him. He'd let down his walls, had let her inside, and he trembled with the force of his desire.

He closed his eyes, tangled his fingers into her hair, and kissed her, really kissed her.

She was his, would never again belong to anyone else—every breath she took, the plea in her eyes, the delicate nectar sliding along his fingers as he dipped the middle one between her legs, it all confirmed she was Landon's.

He threw himself into that kiss.

Her need for Landon consumed her, her hand sliding out from stroking that mouthwatering hardness to now claw all over his back as she pressed closer and kissed him deeper. She couldn't remember wanting a man so much, wanting anything so much.

She gasped when he tore free.

With burning silver eyes, Landon ran his fingertip gently over her trembling lip. His velvety voice sent her into pulsing, surging bliss. "Is this my present, wife?" He stroked her lips and bent his dark head, kissing them gently. "These lips?"

Fevered for his touch, she closed her eyes and purred, having never been spoken to so erotically. "Yes."

She could smell him all around her—cologne and cleanness and desire. He grazed her lips and she felt an incredible rise of sensation and need. The sound, weak, was hers as his hand slid down her back, to grab her buttocks and press her against his hot hard length.

"Are you my present, Beth? Your breasts? Your body?" he whispered fiercely and gathered her closer against him, his weight bearing her down on the bed. He covered her mouth before she could say yes.

She sagged and clung to him as his strong, supple tongue made a path into her mouth. Scalding hot and sweet, he swirled it around hers. Her thighs went liquid as she felt his teeth behind his lips, gently biting her flesh.

She moaned, kissing him back, kissing his throat, his shoulders, her nails biting into his back.

"Need to see…" he murmured against her temple.

He stretched his arm out and flicked the other lamp on. The room burst with even more bright light. Beth gasped and covered her breasts with her hands, crossing her legs, feeling much more vulnerable, totally revealed.

Landon shifted back to take in her image, his lids half-mast across his eyes. "Remove your hands."

Her stomach jumped in her body, her skin on fire, her veins thrumming with heat. "Don't look."

"Remove your hands, Bethany."

"Oh, please," she whispered, knowing she would not be able to resist him.

He grasped her wrists and urged her arms aside, her breasts bared for his eyes. His eyes smoldered at the sight of the creamy globes with the puckered areolas. "You've been hiding from me for weeks. I won't let you hide anymore."

She flushed red, reaching to where her nightgown lay discarded somewhere over the bed, but his hands covered the mounds. "Oh," she gasped.

She sucked in a breath when his thumbs swiped across the nipples.

"Beth, I've wanted to see…" With the heel of his palm, he lifted it to his mouth as he ducked his head. "These lovely babies…" He brushed his lips back and forth. "From the moment I met you." He latched on to one and she shivered. He wrapped his arms around her waist and drew her against his chest. "We make good war, Bethany… Do you love with the same passion you hate?"

She bit her lower lip and clutched the back of his head, her voice a squeak. "No."

"I don't believe you, little wife, I don't believe you one bit."

She shut her eyes. A burst of passion overruled her, greater than hate, greater than anything.

He reached between their bodies to pull the drawstring of his pants open, his arms fully extending as he positioned himself over her once more. He was naked now. As naked as she.

What Landon revealed made her eyes widen and her mouth flood for a taste. His penis strained, enormous and powerful.

"Don't be frightened." He cupped the back of her head and held her imprisoned for his descending lips. She responded to his kiss, drowning in a sea of ecstasy, loving how his arousal rubbed against her stomach. She was swept into a tide of lust as he gently rocked it against her.

A need for him, for feeling him buried into her depths, built and clenched inside her womb.

Her hands roamed and savored the silk of his skin under her fingers, his form solid and heavy and smooth, his jaw deliciously abrading her skin as he nuzzled her breasts. Simple, unadultered lust. It was just that. But it felt like more, like it was everything. A deluge of sensations assailed her.

"I've pictured you like this so many times, Bethany." He reached between her legs and his touch slipped and slid into her. "I pictured you wet…as wet as this. Soaked for me."

She was lost in his eyes, their warmth swirling around her. She surged upward, clutching his shoulders, and scraped her cheeks like a cat against the faint stubble of beard along his jaw.

"Landon." Her fingers then trailed down the furring of dark hair on his chest. His mouth was a flame racing through her skin. Every groan of his surged in her blood like a drug, intoxicating her.

His tone slid like a rasp of silk, low and seductive. "My beautiful wife."

Twisting her head on the pillows, she caught him closer to her, bringing his prominent erection to nestle between her thighs. She parted her legs—a perfect fit. "Please."

He started leaving her, and her limbs clenched around him in panic. "No!"

"Shh. I'm merely getting a condom."

She released him, flustered. "Oh." She stole a glimpse of his rigid stomach, his hair-dusted thighs and calves as he bit the foil packet and tore it open with his teeth. He slid the protection on, and she had never seen anything sexier than Landon's hands, covering his erection. "What?" he persisted with gentle firmness.

She shuddered, pierced with rapture as he sat on the edge of the bed. "Thank you—for remembering about that."

He dragged her over his lap, his hands guiding her legs around his hips. He impaled her slowly, completely, and groaned. His lips locked around her risen nipples and suckled. She bucked as pleasure shot through her. He blew and licked at the peaks, killing her softly. Heat spread through her body, unfurling like ribbons. She heard her moans, their bodies slapping in rhythm. His cheeks were flaming hot, Beth's body perspiring and quivering like a strained bow.

She'd never known anything could be like this, this togetherness existed, this passion, this need and this hunger.

His hips arched into hers hard. Over and over

again. His hands guided her own movements, bouncing her against him. Faster, deeper, with more purpose.

Her body ruled, screamed, opened and closed around him. The burn intensified, the clench in her womb unbearable.

Her cry came first, but the sound he made was greater, so sexy, so low, torn from his chest as he shuddered.

And in that instant it was just him and her, no war, no one else, but Beth and Landon.

Eleven

He wanted to see her.

One night, one long board meeting, three phone calls, one conference call and two coffees later, Landon Gage wanted to see his wife in the middle of the morning.

Holy God, he'd never felt like this. Superhuman, all powerful, complete.

In the six years before her he'd needed nothing but himself. Now it was early morning, and he stood in his office by the sunlit window, remembering how he'd woken up with a warm, snuggly Beth less than four hours ago. His body hungered still, an animal awakened and demanding to take every need and craving not appeased for years. He wanted her again—right now.

But he would not be satisfied with just her body. He wanted something else.

The family he'd been robbed of.

Her trust, her respect, hell, her *love.*

He wanted it.

He'd watched her hair, thick and lustrous, tumble past her shoulders as she lay asleep, and he'd memorized her lips, wet and plump and desirable, and his face had tightened with pent-up need as he stood in his Boss suit, dressed for work and unwilling to leave.

She'd stirred in bed like a sleepy kitten and stretched out her arms above her head, her breasts peeping out from under the covers. He'd never seen anything so beautiful. He wanted to bend over and gently take the pink peaks of her nipples and suckle her, but instead he sat next to her and placed a hand on her hips, caressing her.

"Rough night?" he asked, huskily. He caught her scent in the sheets, mingled with his, and he felt light-headed.

Beth made a sultry sound and rolled to her side to face him. Her smile was endless, her cheeks flushed. "I still think I dreamed it. You?" Her voice was throaty with sleep—he liked it.

The urge to taste her again rippled in his insides. He bent, smelling her, inhaling her, a sensation he recognized as anticipation heating his blood and groin as he kissed her lips. "I've got to go."

She pulled him to her. A prickle of excitement tightened every inch of his body as their mouths tangled, so he kissed her harder. But his thoughts intruded, tormenting his insides. Halifax must be taken care of....

He set himself free. "I've got to go," he repeated, more sternly.

She sat up with a frown, glancing at the clock. "What time is it?"

"Seven-thirty."

He watched her tie the ribbon of her wrinkled gown, and his body screamed for him to rip off his tie and jump back in bed with her.

He forced himself to take several steps to the door. "I pride myself in being the first at the office. I'm late as it is."

Her eyes twinkled with laughter. "So everyone will know you spent last night in bed with me, then."

Only I'll know, he thought. *And I'll know it all day.*

Lust vibrated inside him at the thought, tightening his legs, his groin, as he watched her walk over on those amazing bare legs. "You're my wife," he said, gutturally. "From this moment on, you sleep in my bed."

Instead of protesting, she nodded slowly, which only served to heighten his desire to alarming levels. They'd trusted each other completely, no walls, no deceit. She'd told him things, about how she'd wanted him, and he'd told her things, too.

"Maybe you should stay awhile," she said in a wispy voice, fingering his collar. "And I'll make you breakfast, Landon."

Court hearing, he thought as he gazed fixedly at her soft, delicious mouth. *Need to schedule the court hearing. Then Beth leaves and I go back to the way I was before. No! I won't allow it. She's mine—she's staying with me.* Me.

God, but she was caring and warm and giving. He could stay with her all morning.

But he didn't. He hadn't.

He'd exerted every ounce of willpower, told her to go buy something for court and had made it to the office on time before his brothers. On time to his meetings, to give Beth what she wanted. Her son.

He'd never been so determined to nail Halifax before—as though that one action would make his every unknown dream come true.

From 9:00 a.m. to 11:00 a.m., Landon had closeted himself with his lawyers and brothers to review the evidence they had on Halifax so far. Mason, the attorney at family law, assured him that with the taped confession Julian had wheedled out of Hector's head nurse, the odds were on their side. Not to mention, the staggering evidence of health fraud stacking up on Hector's back. The man was embezzling pharmaceuticals with the help of a wanted Mexican smuggler. He was robbing health insurance companies by duplicating claims, and prescribing expensive, dangerous medications the patients didn't really need.

The guy was a con man, a liar and a fraud with an M.D.

Once they'd finished their discussion and wrapped up their plans, Landon attempted to delve back into work, but kept thinking about the tousled siren he'd left this morning in bed.

He wanted to feel confident about the hearing, but too much rode on that one day, one decision, to find any ease for the stiff muscles in his back. He felt tense, primed like a prized fighting bull—and damned hot at the thought of being with his wife again.

He wanted to see her. Smack in the middle of the day, he wanted to see his wife.

He picked up the phone and dialed the house, but

when Martha mentioned Bethany had gone out with Thomas to the mall, he rang for his assistant.

"Donna, I'm taking an early lunch with my wife. Reroute all my calls."

In the midst of a shopping frenzy, Beth opened the dressing-room door. "Miss, would you happen to have this in—"

Landon's Hermès tie stood an inch from her nose and Beth squeaked and covered herself as if she were naked. She stumbled back. "What are you doing here? Get out!"

"Relax." He stepped inside, shut the door and leaned back on his heels, forehead furrowed as he regarded the skirt and jacket she'd tried on. "Drop your hands, let me see."

Beth dropped her hands, wanting to pull a bag over her face, she felt so red. She forced herself to remain still as his eyes traveled her, lingering in indecent places. The suit was about as secretarial as they came, but she could've been stark naked for the way his eyes regarded her. "Good." He met her gaze with a sarcastic tilt of his lips. "For a woman twice your age, perhaps."

"I need to look respectable for court," she reminded him.

"You can look both young and respectable." Suddenly, he was deeper into the room, prying through the choices that hung to the side. With the bright overhead lights, his face was perfectly clear. Bronze, chiseled, he was a Greek god.

"Can I help you with any sizes?" The saleslady peeped through the shuttered door.

He straightened as though the woman had been speaking to him. He flung the door open and Beth heard a startled gasp. "Yes. Bring my wife something elegant, expensive and unique. Not too showy, well-cut…" He turned his attention to Beth. "Your size?"

"Six."

"Six it is. Anything else, sir?"

He studied the lingerie piled on the corner chair—white—which she had discreetly brought over to try on.

"And lingerie," he added, watching Beth's reaction as he lifted a plain cotton panty up to his line of vision. "Something feminine and smaller than this."

Bethany could find no place to hide, with all the mirrors in the room. She saw four Landons—his back—his profile—his front. All of the sights were quite mesmerizing. His fingers touching the panty was the sexiest thing she'd ever seen.

Landon plopped down on the sole chair and folded

his arms behind his head as the woman came in with an assortment of clothes. Beth dared not look at the prices, but the fabrics were exquisite, the cuts sublime.

All it took was a man in Hugo Boss to say, "Bring something nice," and suddenly, voilà, Chanel was on the rack.

"Akris," the saleslady said of a cream dress with a boat-cut shoulder. "You won't want to take it off. Like second skin, very flattering on." She turned to Landon. "And—" She pulled out bra after bra, panty after panty, of the most decadent lace imaginable. "For your wife."

"Leave them here."

She did, and then asked if Beth needed help with the Akris dress. "It's difficult to button in the back," she explained. "Rows and rows of buttons."

Landon had opened a magazine among a stack on a small table and pretended to be riveted. The saleslady proceeded to help Beth out of the jacket and skirt so she could get into the dress. "I'm used to the men hardly even looking. They've seen everything," she muttered into Beth's ear.

"Yes, but mine is—"

"Gorgeous, darling, oh, goodness, the ladies outside are just waiting to have an eyeful."

Beth frowned. *Oh, were they?* She pretended nonchalance as the woman slipped the Akris dress on and began to work button after button, and when Beth turned, Landon's hot, appreciative gaze hit her like a blast.

"Well," the lady said, patting her back, "what do you think?"

Beth caught her reflection; she looked good, the dress fitting beautifully and making her seem even curvier than she actually was—which in her case was a good thing.

But the opinion both women waited for did not come.

For the longest time, Landon said nothing. Then gruffly, "Leave us, please."

He set the magazine down, and Beth's heart began to thump wildly as the saleslady departed. The dress detailed everything—the soft mounds of her breasts, the peaked nipples, her hips.

"Do you like it, Landon?"

She needed to hear his opinion now, because his gaze made her mind pull this way and that, and her stomach kept fluttering.

He reached out to her waist, inspecting the texture, his features hard with concentration as he considered. He fondled a breast, pushed the mound high in his hand and rubbed gently. "Why did you marry him?"

His touch and all that it caused inside her made it difficult to speak. "I told you. I was young. And pregnant. And stupid—" As she spoke, he looped his fingers through the gold belt around her waist and drew her toward him. As their hips met, their lips met, and she felt him respond, growing harder against her, groaning as he kissed her.

When he stopped, he let out a breath of frustration, and released her. But he did not step back, continued caging her in with his body. He reached around her and plucked open a button, then another. "Why him?"

She reached behind her and tried closing the opening, but his hand was already there, stroking downward. She watched his face contort in hunger. Felt his jealousy, how it was eating at him, burned in his eyes. "He…he did something nice for me. I thought that meant he was a nice person, and I was too young to know better."

He undid a couple more buttons. His big hands trapped her buttocks in each. He kneaded the flesh. "Me buying you clothes is nice. Isn't it?"

"Yes, you—you buy me nice clothes, thank you."

"And yet I'm still the bastard who will help you sink him." His erection scraped against her pelvis and he held her there, his prisoner, and bent his head to let the tip of his tongue dip into her cleavage.

The hot wet heat of his tongue made a sound rise to her throat, a sound of agony. "Yes."

He gripped her bottom tighter and hoisted her up in the air, forcing her legs around him, forcing her to cling as he braced her back against the wall. He caught her earlobe between his teeth, making her toes start to tingle as he nibbled.

She flushed all over. "Landon, don't."

His mouth teased her, approaching hers, retreating then coming closer once again. She shuddered as he pressed into her. Her nails dug into his shoulders.

"Do you see that bit of red over there?" He jerked his head toward the hangers that held all the wicked lingerie.

"Yes."

He touched her cheek with three fingers, stroking downward so sensually she could burst. "I want to know it's under this dress."

"Landon, I don't…"

"Say, 'Yes, Landon'—that's all I want you to say. No one will know. Only me and you. Our own personal little revenge over Halifax." When he moved her arms up high over her head and lowered his head he added, "Let's go out tonight, you and me, Beth."

"You're asking me on a date," she panted, breathless and yet struggling to get free. "Won't our mamas love that."

"I don't care about our mamas. What do you say?"

A laugh escaped her and he broke into a grin, chuckling with her. Her husband. Her wonderful, strong, thirty-three year old husband. On a date.

"Yes."

He kissed her lightly on the forehead before he released her. "You better be ready for me."

But he'd worked Beth so well she thought perhaps her husband should be the one who should be ready for her.

He sent her home with an Akris dress and one very sexy red lingerie set and a mind that whirled and whirled with memories of what they'd almost done in a Neiman Marcus dressing room.

For the rest of the afternoon, she delved into the new "Share Your Recipe" section of the catering website. When the phone rang, she didn't think twice about answering. She lifted it from the desk with a happy "Yes?"

"Outside Maggiano's restaurant at the RIM shopping center. Meet me there in twenty minutes—or you can forget about David."

Halifax hung up.

Twelve

Fear had a strange beat. It slowed down everything—the time, the way Beth's mind processed things. It slowed down everything except her heartbeat. Beth couldn't let Thomas drive her to the restaurant, so she asked for the Navigator, saying she wanted to see her mother, hating to have to lie but too frightened not to.

She made it there in seventeen minutes, but the fear, the gut-wrenching fear, made it seem like years.

These were seventeen minutes of torture where she imagined the worst—David being shipped off somewhere, out of her reach, her touch, forever.

Whatever you do, don't fall apart, Bethany.

Outside the Italian restaurant, under the shadow

of a green tent, Hector lit a cigarette, the tip glowing as he watched her shut the car door and come over.

Heavy clouds gathered above, promising a heavy rain. A family of four exited the restaurant, their cheerful chatter contrasting with the silence with which Hector greeted her.

Beth waited for him to speak first, keenly aware of his potential for violence. But for endless minutes he merely smoked his cigarette and looked her slowly up and down as though he could see Landon's fingertips and brands on her body.

It struck Beth how in six years married to him, she'd never experienced an ounce of the happiness, the connection, she'd felt with Landon in a matter of weeks. How sad that she hadn't known this before, hadn't known that things didn't need to be stale, that things could be better than boring and actually be wonderful.

"You've been talking to Gage," Hector drawled in a hard, insulting voice, putting out his cigarette with his boot. "He's been poking around my business—what did you tell him, Beth?"

She loathed to discover the fear she'd once had of him was still present, crawling up her spine and ready to immobilize her. It was followed with animosity, and hate, so much hate she began to tremble.

"Well, he is my husband. And we do talk, Hector."

It had been a long, long time since she'd spoken to him so firmly.

His eyes became slits, as he gave her the most chilling, most frightening smile. "Your little game has gone on long enough. I say it's time we put a stop to it, don't you? Your mouth has been flapping open for weeks and Beth?" He pitched his voice lower. *"I don't like it."*

Bubbles of hysteria rose to her throat, and she had to swallow before speaking. "The game has only just begun," she said, fighting to sound confident. "I've told him things, Hector. But I've still got to tell him how you medicated his wife until she couldn't even think straight!"

His eyes widened, and he took a threatening step forward. "You wouldn't dare."

"Oh, I dare all right!" She took a step back—and Hector another step forward. "He's on to you, Hector. He knows what you are!"

He manacled her wrist in one hand, his tobacco breath blasting across her face. "One more word out of you and your little husband—"

"You can't hurt him!" she spat, anger and frustration sharpening her voice as she squirmed to free herself. She wanted to shrink from his gaze, his lashing words, his beastly touch. "You've tried for years and you can't touch him!"

His expression contorted into a terrifying sneer. His nails bit into her skin. "Oh, I can hurt him. I'll tear Gage apart if you take me to court, Beth."

She laughed cynically. "Right. Like *you* can destroy a Gage."

Smiling that Lucifer-like smile, he released her. Beth rubbed her wrist as he lighted another cigarette, took a drag, then flicked it down on the ground, and stepped on it. "You're a Lewis." He blew the smoke into her face. "A little nobody. As easily crushed…as this. And Gage…he's scrupulous and it will get him killed. That's no way to win a war, Beth. You'll never get David. Ever."

Her breath grew choppy. Fear and fury whirled and churned in her belly. How could you spend years and years of your life with a rat? How could you bear it?

And Landon. What would he do when she told him about this? He'd warned her not to see him, talk to Hector, but he didn't understand this bastard had her *child!*

"Why do you want him?" she screamed, gripping her purse tight to her chest to keep from flinging it at him. "You hardly paid attention to him. Why do you want him?"

"Because you do." His face was a mask of rage, and his words poison. "Oh, I may have eventually given him back to you, after you learned your lesson of what happens when you leave me. But not after Gage, oh, no, never after Gage. Unless…" Hector snagged her elbow and immediately the space between them disappeared as he stepped forward. "Unless you divorce him and come back to me."

Somewhere in the depths of her panic, she found her courage. She yanked her arm free, and said, "Go to hell."

But he moved fast and he seized her by the arm. This time he cut off her circulation. "Look behind you, Beth. Do you see my blue Lexus parked by the oaks?"

Woodenly, Beth turned, his grip spreading a biting pain up her arm. She saw him. David. His little face pressed against the glass, tears streaming down his cheeks.

Panic choked her.

"David!" she cried, and started for him without thought. Hector yanked her back by both arms and wheeled her around to face him.

He pressed his face inhumanly close, so that when he spoke, she could feel his loathsome lips moving against her own pursed ones. "The only way you can see him and touch him and kiss him is if you return to me. If you return to my bed."

Beth didn't know how she managed, only knew

that she had to leave, now, before this became a public spectacle.

She spat into his face, wrenched free, and ran, her breath soughing out of her chest like a hunted animal's. She flung herself against the side of the Lexus and tried yanking open the door, but it didn't budge. "Mommy!" she heard David wail from the inside, frightened, and her heart broke when she heard the muffled cry coming over and over like a litany.

Tears flowed down her cheeks as she fought with the door. She was crying—crying for him, for her, for every mother.

Helpless to get him out, she put her hand against the window and spread it wide and spoke as loudly as she could. "David, I'm going to be with you soon, I promise! I *promise!*"

And then, before she could notice that David had also spread his palm open on his side of the window, fitting the shape of his small hand into hers, Hector had revved up the engine and sped off with a screech of tires.

Taking her son, her baby, with him once more.

Landon jotted down notes on the legal pad on his desk, then typed the data into his computer. His intercom buzzed, and Donna's voice burst through the speaker.

"Mr. Gage, Detective Harris here to see you."

"Show him in."

His office doors swung open. Harris was a little man with an unremarkable face and a keen eye—the perfect spy. He sat and pulled out a sheaf of papers, matching Landon's brisk manner. "Your wife was out and about today," he said.

Landon's answering smile was brief, cool, as he lifted another file to skim through. "I know. I was with her this morning."

"Well, she seemed to be in a rush to make an appointment this afternoon."

Landon's movements halted. She'd gone out?

When the man remained silent, Landon shot him an impatient look over the top of the report he'd been reading. "And she went where?" Landon set the report aside, and the little man shifted when he gave him his undivided attention.

"To meet Hector Halifax."

Harris dropped the pictures on his desk and Landon's chest muscles froze until he couldn't breathe. He smiled thinly, but inside he experienced something he hadn't felt before. Not in six years. Not ever. He thought he was going to get *sick*. "She went to see Halifax?"

"Indeed."

An instinct to protect her, grab her close to him and never let anyone, much less a rat like Halifax hurt her, warred with the need to grab her little neck and shake some common freaking sense into her.

Why? Why, Bethany, damn it, why?

He gritted his molars in anger. "You must be mistaken," he said.

But Harris rarely was, and signaled at the photographs. "I'm sorry, Mr. Gage. But the pictures speak for themselves."

Landon glared down at them at first, still stunned by the fact that Beth had met Halifax today…

Today, of all days, when they'd at last been granted a hearing date. What she'd done was both reckless and stupid, and finding out this way only poked at the ghosts of a dark, bleak past Landon had long ago tucked away.

Forcing his hand to keep steady, he inspected the pictures on his desk, one by one. This was the second time the man across his desk had brought him this kind of news. The first time, it had enraged him. And now…

His heart stopped at the sight of her in the photographs—the sight of her betraying him.

They were touching… Halifax was touching her… Beth was letting him. His lips were… My God, they were against hers. What was this? What in the hell was *this?*

"Did you witness this yourself?" he demanded.

"I had some blind spots, sir, as I lingered inside the restaurant. But the times they were together, they were close. As you can see."

Landon saw.

Outside, life continued. The office noise. The ringing phones. He set the last picture down and bent his head, his voice rough as tree bark. "What time?"

"This afternoon. 4:30 p.m."

He squeezed his eyes shut against the emotions that assailed him. The thought of the bastard touching her, of Beth standing there while he held her delicate arms, Beth meekly waiting for the kiss to deepen, made Landon want to tear open a wall.

There had been signals, warning bells. Telling him not to trust, not to *want* her. Landon had ignored them, every last one of them. Her meeting Halifax during their engagement party—her resistance to sleeping with Landon.

He hadn't understood why, but he'd forged ahead, first out of revenge perhaps, then out of sheer blind need, pretending he could build something with Beth, something that lasted, something that through the hate and anger and revenge shone special.

Could he have imagined whatever had been grow-ing between them? Could he be that blind? That stupid?

Or had Beth simply thought to sweet-talk Halifax into relinquishing custody?

But Halifax would use this evidence against her.

Growling in frustration, Landon scraped a rough hand down his face, then he and the detective ex-changed a glance that spoke volumes. "Did my wife leave with him?" Landon asked.

"No. When I exited the restaurant, she was getting into her own car."

But not before they'd *kissed!*

Rage stiffened his muscles, gripped his throat, made it hard to speak. Beth's pretty profile in the photo blurred as his vision went red. Halifax. Once again, the bastard thought he could take his wife away from him.

And Beth had gone to him. Despite Landon's warnings, despite how delicate the situation was.

She'd run to the enemy and cast Landon into a role he'd sworn never to be cast in ever again: the fool.

Beth was waiting in the living room, listening to the patter of rain while the dogs slept by the dark fireplace, when she heard Landon's car pull up in the driveway.

After chewing most of her nails off wondering how to describe her encounter with Hector, she felt so glad to see Landon walk through that door, his hair wet, rivulets sliding down his jaw, tiredly dropping a portfolio at his feet, that she flung herself against him and eagerly pressed her mouth to his. "Thank God you're home!"

Stiff and unresponsive, Landon set her aside and commanded the dogs to back off.

Stunned, Beth watched him carry his portfolio over to the desk where he kept his agenda. He set it down on the surface with a thump. "Do you have anything you wish to tell me, Beth?"

He trapped her gaze, and her already-wrung heart seemed to die a sudden death.

She sensed something was wrong.

All around Landon—her husband, her lover, her new best friend—was a wall, emitting a signal to stay away.

The romantic fantasies she'd been entertaining, the ones of kissing him and loving him before she confessed she'd seen Hector, were destroyed by this harsh reality.

Landon was as closed to her as she'd ever seen him.

Tight-lipped, he retrieved a folder from the inside

of the leather case. With an impenetrable look in his eyes, he went to the small bar and prepared a drink. "Cat got your tongue?" he prodded, file in one hand as he poured with the other.

"What's wrong with you…?" Beth asked, confused and wide-eyed. "And what's with the file?"

As he brushed past her, he put the folder in her hand. He fell into the chair behind a small desk with his drink in hand, and said, "Open it."

Beth's hands trembled as she obeyed.

It wasn't the tone he'd used, icy with contempt, or the way he held himself unapproachable as he sat there that unnerved her. It was the look in his eyes.

He knew.

"Recognize the woman in those photographs, dear wife?"

She stared at them and almost keeled over.

The images were staggering, images of her and Hector, speaking and arguing and *kissing.* The bile rose to her throat as she tossed the photos aside. "It's not how it looks, Landon."

Landon smiled, deceptively. Beth opened her mouth to explain more but was dazzled by the gleam of his eyes, stormy with something raw and masculine. Storming with *jealousy.*

Beth could almost hear the trust between them shattering like glass.

Oh, God, what had she done?

"I promise you, Landon, it's not how it looks." With legs that felt ready to buckle, she approached the desk one step at a time and struggled to find the words. But the words seemed to tumble one after the other, fighting to come forth. "He insisted on seeing me, and I needed to know what he wanted. I didn't…kiss him. He forced me. He… Landon, I didn't kiss him."

All expression left his face, but his eyes blazed hot enough to incinerate her. "And what did he want? Huh, Beth? You?"

It hurt to speak. "Yes," she said tightly. *But I'd rather die.*

Lightning struck outside. Rain slammed against the windows, and the howl of the wind echoed in the household. Like the night Landon's first wife died, the night Hector abandoned Beth to meet her; the weather was just as tempestuous and volatile tonight.

Beth felt a worse kind of storm brewing inside her. Fury. It came with a vengeance, overpowering her. She leapt forward as though she'd just been unleashed from captivity and pushed her finger into Landon's chest as he leapt to his feet, too. "How dare you spy on me, how dare you! I did nothing wrong. I'm not…I'm not Chrystine! My baby is with that beast. How can you expect me to not do anything?"

He caught her finger in his hand. "I told you to stay away from him, Beth!"

Her chin jerked up in defiance. "I'm a mother and I'd do anything for my child! What about you, huh? Are you even *helping* me? Or do you conveniently find obstacles in order to keep me around to slake your lust?"

He scoffed. "Slake my lust, that's what you call it?"

"That's what it is! What else would I call it?"

"I didn't slake my lust with you last night, Beth. I made love to you. Love, damn you!"

"Well, excuse me if it doesn't feel like it!" she lied.

Making a sound of frustration, he flung her hand aside as if she'd singed him and drained his glass in one long gulp.

Breathless with fury and emotion, Beth cradled her finger to her chest with one hand, hating that it tingled after he'd grasped it, and when he remained quiet, she shook her head.

"I'm your revenge, Landon, why don't you just admit it!" she cried. "Tit for tat. A wife for a wife."

He'd been so insistent about getting her in bed, she just knew it was his personal war against Hector.

She heard a faint click outside and saw a sudden flash of light then…thunder.

Landon moved far away from her, to the opposite side of the room. He put a hand up to the window as he watched it rain. A strange gravity entered his voice. "Then the joke's on me."

The tension thickened between them, black like tar in an equally black silence.

The clock ticked under the staircase.

She gazed at his wide broad back. She was so angry and at the same time so in love her throat hurt. Inside she felt dark, dark and lost. She was paralyzed, shattering in panic. Because she loved him. And suddenly it felt like he would never return that love.

"Why did you let him touch you, Beth. Do you miss his touch? Do you want it?" he asked raggedly.

"No!" She gasped, aghast that he would think it.

"You rejected mine all this time because it was him you wanted? Did you pretend I was him last night? When you came for me did you—"

"Stop it, stop it!"

His head fell forward, against the window, and he shook his head ruefully. "Why don't you *trust* me?" he hissed.

"I do, Landon, I *do*. I was frightened. I had to know my son was okay. I was helpless all my life, standing like a good little wife by his side. I don't want to be that person anymore!"

He whipped around and pointed a finger. "You're not his wife anymore, Beth, you're mine. My wife!" he thundered.

"I *know* that!" she shouted back.

"Then aren't I entitled to know my wife is meeting my mortal enemy? I vowed to protect you, Bethany—you and your son. My God! That man, that bastard takes my first wife, and he thinks he can take my second?"

She sucked in a gust of air, for the first time realizing that he'd not only been concerned for her safety, but he was terribly jealous, too. And he was speaking of her as a real wife. Touched in places no one in her life but Landon had ever touched before, she lowered her voice. "I'm all right," she said, so vaguely she wondered if he'd heard her. "And I'm not going anywhere."

He met that with silence.

Dark, emotionless silence.

"I didn't kiss him," she repeated, her voice threatening to crack. Landon's face was twisted in torment, and Beth felt twisted on the inside. "Hector wanted me to…to go back to him. I froze when I saw David in the car, watching us, but I swear to you when Hector pulled me close I shut my mouth tight and I—"

Landon growled so angrily, so deeply, so possessively, she fell quiet.

The wind rattled the window casements. Beth shook with the urge to set things right, but she didn't know how. "I spat at him," she continued, after a moment. "It felt amazing, it did...until he drove away with David."

She made a choked sound at the memory and put her arms around herself.

Revenge had been so simple once. Now Landon thought her a liar, as vile as Halifax, as vile as Chrystine had been, and the thought of being compared to them in his mind distressed her.

"I didn't kiss him," she insisted, staring down at the floor when looking into his accusing eyes became unbearable. "Please believe me."

"Those pictures, Beth—" his voice was low, weary "—could be used against us at court if he ever finds them. He painted you as a Jezebel once—he'll do it again."

She gathered her fortitude and met his gaze. "I don't care what anyone thinks as long as you believe me."

Watching her, he plunged his hands into his pants pockets as though he didn't know what to do with them. "What we need is to convince the judge you're a good woman, Beth."

She made a distressed sound and flung her hands up in the air. "He threatened me! He grabbed me! I yanked away when I could. What was I supposed to do!"

"I'm going to *goddamned kill him*."

Stunned by the words, Beth blinked.

Landon cursed and approached, the concern and anger etched across his face making her hope soar. "Did he hurt you?" he demanded.

Beth held her breath as his hands briskly sailed down the front buttons of her shirt, unbuttoning and parting the material, then she gasped when he shoved the material down her shoulders and arms until it dangled from one of her wrists.

Dying with lust, she stood meek as Landon frowned and studied her, skimmed his fingers along her throat, the tops of her arms, her elbows. The skin was unmarked. He expelled a relieved breath and met her gaze, a look of male awareness settling in his eyes.

When he cursed low in his throat and left her standing there, struggling to rearrange her clothes, she'd never felt so cold, so abandoned and rejected.

"I had a child once," he began, his ragged words gaining force as he turned around, "and if you cared for yours as much as you say you do, you'd have played it safe and *stayed away* from Hector Halifax, Bethany."

"He wasn't even your son, Landon!" she screamed, out of her wits with fury over his accusations, his blindness. Didn't he know, damn him? Couldn't he see she was achingly, painfully in love with him? She hadn't kissed Hector. All she wanted, needed, was Landon's support tonight, not his accusations.

The tomb-like silence that followed her cry shattered when Landon spoke.

His timbre was dangerously, warningly soft. "What did you just say?"

Beth lowered her voice. "He was Hector's son. He wasn't yours."

His hands balled and his arms trembled and then, *then* he made a low, terrible sound that tore through her like a knife cut.

That's when it struck her. When the horrible words she'd said dawned on her. What she'd said, how she'd said it, angrily, meant to hurt him.

"Landon, I'm sorry, I—" When she reached out for him, he cursed and stepped aside, giving her his back. "Landon, I didn't mean it like this. It's just that Hector demanded a DNA test before he and Chrystine ran away. I saw the results. He's the father. They fooled around for years, he and Chrystine. They loved making each other jealous. They married us to spite each other off, Landon. Chrystine loved to rub it in Hector's nose how she was able to snag you when you were the best catch—"

His smile grew chillier, and he began to laugh, holding up a hand to stop her. "Don't. Say anymore."

Stopped by that cynical sound, Beth helplessly stood a few feet away, and the ground under her feet had never felt so perilous. What had she done?

Her throat was so clogged she barely heard her own voice, which sounded strangled when she spoke. "I realize I should've told you before, about your son."

"You knew, all this time. You knew about my son and you let me think…you let me talk to you about him…you—"

"It makes no difference!" she cried.

He roared and slammed his chest with one fist. "It makes a difference to *me!*"

He'd still been holding his drink in his other hand, and a slosh of whiskey splashed onto the carpet. Cursing, Landon drained what was left and set the empty glass on the desk, then he stared into its depths.

She considered how she'd take it if someone came up to her and told her David wasn't her son.

How she'd feel if *Landon,* a man whose respect she wanted, had told her this news in the same way Beth had told him.

She shrunk inside her skin, feeling so small.

"I'm sorry, Landon," she said, her voice small, too.

Her eyes welled up for the second time today. She was afraid the tears wouldn't stop until morning.

She didn't know where she found the courage to speak. "Where d-do we stand now? With us? With…David?"

He wouldn't tear his gaze off that empty glass. "I said I'd get you your son back. And I will."

And us?

She couldn't ask it again—somewhere deep down, she knew. Could hear the word "divorce" as clearly as she heard the thunder.

They'd become each other's enemies.

Thirteen

"Pretend you love me well and hard or by God this will blow up in our faces!"

Landon hissed the words into her ear, and a hot shiver raced down Beth's spine. Her nerves were stretched taut in a combination of anticipation and fear.

This was the day she'd been waiting for.

Her heart pounded a nervous beat as she gazed around the space they'd been appointed. The courtroom was exactly the one in her earlier trial: impersonal and cold.

The judge's seat above them loomed empty while their lawyer busily shuffled his notes. His name was Mason Dawson, a young, ruthless attorney already reaping the benefits of his killer reputation. He had assured Beth and Landon every time they met that he didn't lose.

Beth prayed his winning streak wouldn't end with her.

Hector's lawyer, on the other hand, sat at the table on the opposite side, stealing glances at her wristwatch. It was a smart choice to have a woman represent him—someone female to soften his image.

Beth's parents, Mrs. Gage, Garrett, Julian John, Kate and even Thomas had settled themselves in the benches.

But what Beth was most aware of, with every atom, cell and fiber in her body, was the man at the table beside her.

Landon fairly reeked of fury. He stood tall and solid to her right, a tower of testosterone that pricked her body with awareness.

She couldn't help but think of the Akris dress she wore, the underwear she wore beneath. Would Landon even attempt to discover if she'd worn the red lingerie like he'd told her to?

God, she was lovesick. Or just sick.

"He's late," their lawyer muttered to them.

Just then, the doors burst open, and Hector appeared.

He looked like a man who'd just had an encounter

with a rabid lion and had barely come out of it on his feet.

He stumbled forward, a dark coffee stain on his olive green coat. His hair was rumpled, his face streaked with dirt as though he'd tripped in a mud puddle.

He whipped off his coat as he went to his table, his cheeks flushed with two bright red flags. His lawyer, concerned, immediately rose, and he bit out, "I'm fine! Just an inconvenience." He glared in Landon's direction.

Beth frowned, her eyes sailing to his inscrutable profile.

Had Landon somehow planned Hector's...inconvenience?

The object of her wondering edged closer to her, and the back of his long fingers grazed her knuckles, the contact as sudden as it was exquisite. Landon prolonged that touch, and finally snatched up her hand in his.

Her knees turned to jelly, and a lump of emotion lodged in her throat. She could cry. She knew he held her hand for appearances, pretense, and yet she squeezed and curled her fingers through his and held on to him like a lifeline.

His breath stirred the hair on top of her head, and when she trembled slightly, he laced his fingers tighter through hers. His voice softened. "Relax. Look confident."

Beth tried. This was not the moment to get emotional, to dwell on the past horrible weeks. But she couldn't stop weeping inside.

There was no removing that sensation, that horrible sensation of having been hanged. Stabbed in the chest. Or shot.

She'd hurt him in the worst possible way, and now Landon hated her.

She stiffened when the judge appeared in a swish of robes. He was a bald man with a beard, a determined set to his jaw, and clear eyes.

"Ladies and gentlemen, this court is now in session. The Honorable Judge Prescott presiding. All rise."

Beth's mind whirled with images of David's toothy grin, memories of how his face had been streaked with tears the last time she'd seen him, and her heart felt ready to implode. She may have nothing, she realized, straightening her spine, but she fought for everything.

When she stood up, she met Halifax's sparkling blue gaze—icy cold. She made her own expression glacial.

Together, her parents and Landon's group crowded the two front rows on their side. They presented a united front, a respectable family. Standing so close and so proud, the Gages emitted that same power Landon did.

But…why was that not reassuring?

Because without Landon's respect, Beth felt apart, not one of them. Because without Landon's interest in her, the caring way he'd protected her before, she felt…fraudulent.

Like Hector.

"Your Honor," Mason began in a crisp opening statement. "I stand before you today on behalf of my clients, Landon and Bethany Gage, with a petition for full custody of David Halifax. Landon Gage has been an upstanding citizen of this community for the past thirty-three years. His wife, Bethany Gage, has been outrageously accused in the past—and has suffered a great injustice. A mother. Robbed of the opportunity to give love and affection and participate in the raising of her son."

A dramatic pause ensued while Mason raked the courtroom with his eyes, continuing only when convinced everyone's focus lay on him.

"I beg you to consider today, who is the better custodian? A father who's suspected of fraud, a father whose very nature of work keeps him long hours at the office, such as Dr. Hector Halifax? Or a solid, upstanding couple, a well-respected businessman and a dedicated mother whose guidance is indispensable to a young child David's age?"

He allowed the question to linger before he resumed his seat in dramatic silence, and Hector's lawyer opened her own statement with a receding chuckle.

"Your Honor, Dr. Hector Halifax's reputation is pristine. His entire life he's been dedicated to the well-being of others, especially his own son. Should a man be punished for loving and protecting his child from his mother's neglect? Should a man who has nurtured and cared for young David during the past year be discriminated against for being a single parent?" She glared at Bethany. "Considering the petitioner's numerous love affairs while she was married to my client, I doubt her marriage to Mr. Gage will even last long."

The petitioner, in this case Beth and Landon, was the first to call up a witness. Beth.

She took a series of measured steps to the stand, inhumanly aware of the sexy lingerie that hugged her body under the dress. She sat and concentrated on inhaling, in and out, in and out. But for the way she truly felt, she could've been naked and strapped to an electric chair.

"Mrs. Gage, how long were you married to Hector Halifax?"

Beth focused on Mason's striped tie. That lone, harmless tie was the only spot she would allow herself to focus on.

"Almost seven years."

"Were you happy during those seven years, Mrs. Gage?"

She wrung her hands. "I was happy when our son was born."

Mason thoughtfully paced the floor before her. Playing the game she supposed all lawyers played, he allowed her heart to beat three times before he spoke again. "Were you happy during the remainder of those years?"

"No."

Mason swung round to face her fully. "No. You weren't happy married to Hector Halifax." He approached, his expression as intent as his voice. "Can you tell the court why you were unhappy?"

Skewered under not only Mason's sharp brown gaze, but also a dozen others, Beth struggled to find a starting point.

"Did he physically abuse you, Mrs. Gage?" Mason leaned back on his heels and waited. "Was he unfaithful?"

She seized her cue, almost leaping. "Yes. He was unfaithful."

Mason stole a brief glance in the judge's direction.

"Hector Halifax was unfaithful to you. When did you decide to leave him?"

"When I realized he'd loved another woman all the time he'd been married to me. And when I realized I didn't love him anymore, maybe never really had."

"How did Hector take it? Your separation?"

Aware of Hector's eyes burning holes through the top of her head, she wouldn't give him the satisfaction of looking at him.

"We had several failed attempts to separate, but he persuaded me to stay. I was only successful when David turned six. Over a year ago."

"Did his method of persuading you to remain married include blackmail, Mrs. Gage? Perhaps… in the way of these pictures? Presented to court during your first hearing?"

Beth spotted a wad of pictures in Mason's hands, and the humiliation she felt threatened to overwhelmed her. Just to think of Landon seeing those pictures of her in different men's embraces, even if they were fake, made her stomach roil. "Yes, that did play a part. And of course, he threatened to take David away."

"Your Honor, may I present for evidence both the pictures *and* lab report which concludes these photographs have been tampered with?"

The judge received the stack of pictures and the lab paper Mason produced and reviewed them in tense silence. Beth squirmed in her seat, part of her wishing she'd had such a kick-butt lawyer on her side the last time she'd been in court, and another part dreading what came next. Hector's lawyer looked so pale and pissed Beth was sure she was going to be that woman's lunch.

Mason continued the interrogation, his questions expertly phrased in ways that shed light on the good, caring mother she was. A loving wife who hadn't been properly appreciated by her first husband.

Her nervousness escalated when the topic led to the new man in her life. Landon. To speak of Landon and Hector in the same conversation almost felt like blasphemy.

Beth struggled to put up a brave front, an image of a new family, but in the deepest, darkest part of her, she knew what she said was a lie every bit as bad as those Halifax loved making. She didn't offer a wonderful new family and a new father to David—she offered only herself and her love.

Suddenly, it didn't feel like enough next to the Gages.

It didn't feel like enough next to the protection, the safety Landon represented.

Everything he'd promised he'd do for Beth, he

had. Whatever the verdict, Landon Gage had come through for Beth.

He'd gotten her a new hearing.

And what had *she* done for *him?*

Her throat felt crowded with unspoken words and remorse for how she'd hurt him. She hadn't been his wife who'd betrayed him, who'd abandoned him one rainy night, but she felt like she was—because she'd opened his eyes and he loathed her for it.

Her spirits plummeted when Mason finished off his questioning, and now the other lawyer's turn came up. Beth braced herself for the attack. The female lawyer's eyes glimmered as she approached, not even bothering to hide the fact that she enjoyed every second of Beth's anxiety.

"Mrs. Gage, tell me one thing," the smooth-talking woman began. "Why did you marry Landon Gage? Was it because you needed to clean up your image? Or because of his money?"

Mason slammed a hand down. "Objection, Your Honor!"

"Objection sustained."

"Your Honor," the defense argued, adding a winning smile to drive her point home, "her motivations for the marriage are dubious, at best, especially so soon after her divorce from Mr. Halifax. I insist

Mrs. Gage give us a direct answer to a direct question. Why did you marry Mr. Gage?"

Beth waited for someone to object, her dread escalating.

No one objected.

"I'll allow it," the judge conceded, sighing. "Answer the question."

Frantic, her eyes searched a pair of familiar gray ones across the room. The instant her gaze locked with Landon's, her chest exploded with emotion. "I love him," she said, lowering her face as the words, so true and so audible, trickled into her own ears.

"Mrs. Gage, please speak up, we couldn't—"

"I love him. I love Landon."

Landon stiffened as though the truth had been a lie, the confession a slap.

Peering at him through her lashes, Beth's hopes of forgiveness were pulverized. His jaw hardened, and his eyes flashed with accusation. The look in his eyes destroyed her confidence. *Pretend you love me well and hard or by God this'll blow up in our faces,* he'd said.

He thought she was pretending!

"You say you love your husband, and yet my client mentions you've been speaking of a reconciliation?"

Her stomach felt so cramped she thought she'd vomit. "There's no reconciliation."

"Mrs. Gage…" Hector's lawyer lifted a shiny flat object in her hand. She lengthened the moment until the curiosity to discover what she held up for inspection ate at Beth on the inside—like the attorney surely intended it to. "When was this picture taken? Contrary to your attorney's claims on the former pictures, this one is fully authentic, is it not?"

Her entire world, her entire perfect world which consisted of her enjoying a lifetime of full and complete custody of David, seemed to crumple as she gazed down at the photograph. Somehow, these people had managed to produce a new set of photographs from the meeting at Maggiano's. God! How many of these vulgar folks had been watching them? How many cowards had stood there, snapping pictures while her life fell apart, and done nothing to help her?

Outraged, Beth scrutinized the close-up of Hector's lips a breath away from hers. Landon had known this would occur. He'd warned her. He'd told her not to go, and one morning over coffee, she'd agreed.

Then she'd gone to meet that stinking rat Halifax anyway.

And guess what? Landon had been right, and Beth had been utterly *wrong*.

Flustered and blushing a disturbing shade of red,

Beth met the woman's hard stare head-on. "Hector called and said I wouldn't be able to see my son if I didn't meet him. You can check the phone records."

"As a matter of fact, I have. Wasn't that you calling from Mr. Gage's home the afternoon of your engagement party?"

"I was calling my son!" Beth burst out, then quickly caught herself and pursed her lips.

Calm. She had to stay *calm.*

The questioning continued; and each lashing sentence pounded her like a sledgehammer. Had she committed infidelities as well? Did she have proof of this supposed infidelity her first husband had committed? Had she written this love note? A love note! A lie, a prefabricated piece of evidence, like those Hector loved to produce.

Beth, upon a silent glare from Mason, limited her answers now to yes and no. Most were no. No, no infidelities, no love note, no reconciliation, until the lawyer tired and allowed Mason to call his next witness.

Landon took the stand.

It seemed that even time stood still in a show of appreciation for his lithe, powerful walk. Beth observed him as she resumed her place at the table, inwardly wanting to sigh. Every sharp plane of his face fascinated her; the arrogant slant of his nose, the raw power in his jaw and the dark shadow across it. She would not look at his thick, fat, plump, delicious mouth, or she would never be able to concentrate.

Mason kept his interrogation brief, but Beth perked up in interest when Hector's lawyer approached to question Landon. If someone could put that hateful woman in her place, it might as well be him.

"Mr. Gage, do you have children?"

His hard, sinewy muscles rippled as he folded his long arms over his chest. He leaned back with such a look of calm that could make even Hector's glares look less chilling. "No."

"Have you ever had children?"

Beth's chest muscles tightened at the knife-edged question. Landon, expressionless, allowed the attorney to wait for a moment before he answered her. "I had a son."

"And where is your son now, Mr. Gage?"

My God, was the woman even human? Beth was furious on Landon's behalf and trembled with the impulse to charge up there and tear the attorney's eyeballs out. No one could know how painful it was to Landon to speak of this boy, except Beth. "He passed away when he was ten months old," Landon tersely replied.

The judge's expression broke with empathy as he regarded Landon.

"Tell me, Mr. Gage. Is David your son?" the attorney asked.

"He's my wife's son."

"And my client's son?"

"Correct."

The lawyer paced thoughtfully. "When did you meet your wife?"

Landon told them when. She asked, not without a hint of sarcasm, "A confirmed bachelor for so long, with your choice of women, why marry one with such a 'reputation'?"

Mason lifted the pen he used to make notes. "Objection, Your Honor, she's slandering my client."

"Sustained."

The perturbing laugh the woman released only made Beth's fury escalate. "I must rephrase. Mr. Gage, why did you marry Bethany Halifax?"

Mason flew to his feet this time, slamming down a hand. "Objection, Your Honor! Mrs. Gage is insulted by the deliberate use of her old name and I must ask that it be stricken from the record."

"Sustained," the judge conceded.

Now, the opposing attorney set her jaw in determination and walked so close to Landon, Beth had to angle to the side to see his face. "Do you love your wife, Mr. Gage?"

Landon's gaze flicked to hers. He lowered his voice to a rough whisper, and although he wore an expression of cold indifference, his eyes gleamed with intensity as he stared at Beth. "Yes."

If Beth had just been torpedoed, the impact would have been less than that single word.

"How do you feel about this picture, Mr. Gage?"

A shadow crossed Landon's eyes as he inspected the photograph she showed him—no doubt the same disgusting, humiliating photograph she'd shown to Beth. "Enraged," Landon said, his low, silken voice laced with a threat.

"Why does it enrage you?"

"Because Halifax exploits the fact that my wife loves her child—and will go to any lengths to blackmail and hurt her."

The lawyer seemed vaguely amused as though she couldn't fathom where Landon got such an idea, then asked plainly, "Do you hate Hector Halifax, Mr. Gage?"

The question hung in the air for a tense moment. Sirens wailed inside Beth's head, a warning.

"Do you admit, Mr. Gage, that *you* hate Hector Halifax and would do anything to hurt him? Would go to *any lengths* to ruin him?"

Silence.

Beth held her breath until her lungs burned, mentally willing him to deny this accusation. If he didn't, they would be doomed. But then she knew Landon, and she knew that Landon Gage did not lie....

Then a hard, murderous word resounded in the room, spoken without apology or hesitation. "Yes." Mason cursed quietly at Beth's side, while Landon continued. "I hate Halifax. And I *will* ruin him."

Hector's attorney smiled in victory, then waved an arm out as though that were that. "No more questions, Your Honor."

The second day of the hearing, Landon again held Beth's hand.

His grip was warm and strong, offering much-needed support as they watched Hector take the stand. While she put every effort into reining back her nervousness and her bleak thoughts of the day ahead, Landon looked eerily calm today.

The men had been locked in Landon's study all through last night, and it seemed that whatever last minute evidence Landon had provided made the lawyer conspiratorially tell Beth this morning, "It's in the bag."

Beth had no idea what the men planned to accomplish today, but as the hearing got underway, when Hector's head nurse and primary character witness was being questioned, Beth prayed they had a plan.

Because the head nurse somehow managed to make it sound like the bastard was on his merry way to being canonized.

"He's been a good father, completely dedicated to providing for his son…" the head nurse was saying. A tidy woman, she had clear skin, little makeup, a bun at her nape that did not have so much as a hair out of place. Her hands remained clasped over her lap as she spoke.

Mason didn't seem impressed.

"Dr. Halifax provides his son with what, exactly?" he asked her, addressing the court first, then the woman. "Money? Or time, love and comfort, as his mother did?"

The head nurse bit her lower lip.

"Your Honor," Mason then said, when the woman didn't answer, "may I submit for evidence this recording of the witness speaking."

Before Beth could register what happened, a small tape recorder played, and the nurse's eyes went huge as a voice remarkably like hers rang out.

Oh, yes, he's horrible in that respect. He's cheap with money, cheap with praise, cheap with everything. We have photocopies of patient records and submit them twice for insurance payment. All I do is change the patient's name...

Murmurs erupted in the courtroom. Astounded whispers.

Patients are so paranoid, it's so laughable. If the doctor tells them there's a miracle drug that will cure all their troubles, most will jump in without question—they're addicted to the medical marijuana the doctor's supplying. It's such good stuff, do you want a little hit?

The courtroom whispers escalated to shocked voices.

"Tell me, Miss Sanchez," Mason broke in in a booming voice. "Is that you speaking?"

"Objection on the grounds of irrelevance, Your Honor!" Hector's lawyer cried, hands on the table.

"Overruled," the judge said. "Sit down, counselor."

Landon gave Beth a reassuring hand-squeeze as the nurse shifted uncomfortably in her seat, a bug under the microscope. Her eyes sought out Julian John's in the benches, and Beth puzzled to see her brother-in-law shoot the woman a winning, you're-screwed smile. The kind of smile the cat would give the mouse. "Yes. It's my voice," she admitted, shooting daggers at Julian, who didn't seem to mind at all.

"Is that you speaking about Dr. Halifax?"

"I…yes."

"Is that you referring to Dr. Halifax committing insurance fraud in order to 'provide' for his lavish lifestyle while negligent of his child?"

"Uh, well—"

"Is that you *admitting* to Dr. Halifax's numerous *illegal* activities, in which you've played a part?"

"But I was only—"

"Is that you, Miss Sanchez, speaking from first-hand knowledge about Dr. Halifax being engaged in *medical malpractice* and the *illegal* prescription of *medical marijuana?*"

She lowered her face as though she wanted to bury it under her sweater. "Yes."

Mason allowed the answer to echo in the room until it faded into a charged quiet. Then, curtly, with a pleased nod, he said, "No more questions, Your Honor."

When Hector was called up to the stand, the air of the courtroom became charged with hostility. His own lawyer interrogated him first, asking him questions about his son, making suggestions that hinted at his being a loving father when Beth knew that was not the case at all! How could she have ever married him? How could she have thought that whatever childish infatuation she'd felt for him could be love? What she felt for Landon defied even comparison—an ocean compared to a grain of sand.

When Mason got to have his go at the man, he had a take-no-prisoners expression on his face. He lifted a piece of paper for all to see. The court, the judge and then the witness.

"Is this your email, Dr. Halifax?"

Hector didn't so much as glance at the page. "Possibly."

"Yes or no, Dr. Halifax. Did you write this email to a patient of yours, Chrystine Gage?"

"Yes," Hector tightly conceded.

"And is this you, Doctor, threatening not to hand out any more prescriptions to your patient unless she did what you commanded?"

"I was merely—"

"Is it or is it not you, *threatening* a patient?"

"Yes," he ground, through clenched teeth.

Mason shook his head in bleak disapproval. "What drug was your patient on?"

"I don't remember."

"Your Honor." Mason produced a new piece of evidence. "We have a prescription from Dr. Halifax made out to Chrystine Gage two days before her death for a drug called Clonazepam.

"Isn't Clonazepam prescribed not only as an anti-anxiety medication, but also as a sleeping pill?"

Hector was silent.

"Isn't it risky for a patient to drive under the influence?"

Hector still didn't respond.

"The witness will answer the counselor," the judge commanded.

"Yes, the drug can be used as a sleeping pill!" Hector grumbled. "Driving is not recommended while using it."

"And yet that is *precisely* what you were demanding your patient do—that she drive to a lonely parking lot in the middle of the night to meet you. That is what your patient ultimately did, resulting in the crash that killed her and her young boy. You *killed* a ten-month-old baby, Dr. Halifax. You *killed* a mother and her child—what's there to recommend you for taking care of your own child?"

"Objection, Your Honor!"

"Overruled. The witness's comment on this is relevant. *Answer.*"

Hector scowled at Beth, the blatant fury in his gaze palpable as a tornado.

He began shaking, visibly shaking in his seat, and burst out, *"You."* He trained his finger like a gun on Beth's forehead, and his mocking tone felt like shards of glass scraping down her skin. "You're worse than I am! Who do you think you are, you little tramp?"

"Silence!" The judge hammered.

Hector's face contorted as he stood, his stormy, furious blue eyes tempting Beth to curl herself into a ball. "You think you can come here and humiliate me?"

"Counselor! You will silence your witness or I'll hold you both in contempt!" Furious now, blue veins stuck out on Judge Prescott's neck.

Hector fell quiet, chastised and displeased, but Mason wasn't yet done with him.

The little black book came up for showing. In the book were Hector's contact numbers for Miguel Gomez, the man who smuggled the illegal marijuana Hector had been sticking to his patients. Also in the book were the numbers of several bribed members of the press who'd promptly been fired not only by the *Daily*, but from the competition as soon as their questionable activities had been reported. Stumbling over his denials, Hector ended up, unwillingly, admitting to all the allegations Mason presented.

By the time he left the stand, her ex-husband looked like an unstable madman, unfit for being a doctor or a parent, while Landon sat quietly beside her, the epitome of the somber businessman.

Scrambling to get back the upper hand, Halifax's lawyer called up the last witness. The entire case now hinged on the nanny.

Anna took the stand, and once she settled in the seat, she made eye contact with Beth.

Hector's lawyer interrogated her on Hector's parenting. Anna answered the questions easily at first, but she kept glancing at Beth, as though waging some sort of silent battle inside herself. Her answers seemed to be limited to "yes" and "no," but she spoke them as though they were wrenched and squeezed out of her by force.

When it was Mason's turn, he first asked her basic questions about her role in raising David. He seemed to barely be getting warmed up when her eyes scanned the room, took in the sight of Landon's family, then returned to Beth, and she blurted, "I can't do this," in a wild and frantic voice.

Like a predator spotting his prey's weakness, Mason jumped at her. "What is it you can't do? Continue working for Dr. Halifax? Continue allowing this injustice—"

"All of it. I can't do it anymore!" Her eyes welled up, and her voice broke as she continued, slightly calmer, "They promised…I'd live well for the rest of my life. As a token of appreciation from the doctor, if I testified. The nanny who testified previously is no longer working at the home. She took the money they gave her to testify last time, and now there's just me. I've been promised a good education for my son, you see. He's almost David's age…" She trailed off and swallowed, as though the next words proved difficult to say.

"But I can't bear to watch this anymore. The child shouldn't be punished like he has been. David needs his *mother*. There's only so much a nanny can give him, and he gets none of it from the doctor. The boy needs his *mother*."

Tears pricked Beth's eyes, and she quickly delved into her bag in search of her tissues. She hadn't expected the nanny to come through for her like this, but then maybe, just maybe, there were more good, decent people in this world than bad ones.

Whispers spread across the room. Hector jumped to his feet and called the nanny a liar, and the judge moved his hammer as he demanded silence.

During recess, Beth wiped the moisture from her cheeks and sat with Landon on a small bench out in the hall. "I'm sorry," she said, clenching her damp tissue in her fist. "That must have been difficult for you. Talking about Chrystine and…"

"Nathan." Landon's timbre dropped to a rough whisper. "His name was Nathan."

The pressure mounted in her chest. She nodded. Nathan.

Imagine Landon as a father. He'd be such a great father. Great brother. Great husband. Oh, God, would he ever trust her again? He was a just man but she suspected he wasn't a forgiving one.

Feeling faint and pale, Beth smiled exhaustedly at him. "You talked to Anna, didn't you?"

"We made sure the court knew what a scumbag Hector is, but we didn't talk to her, Beth. That was all your doing. Clearly she respects you."

The words, somehow, seemed a compliment.

She hesitated, then edged closer, desperate to again reach places she'd reached in him before. "Do you think we'll win?"

He continued absently staring at the crowded hall before them. "We'll win."

She wanted to say something, but felt emotionally drained. Still, she attempted something light and funny, even though she didn't feel like laughing. "Lucky you, you'll be getting rid of me soon."

He turned to her then, and the lack of emotion in his eyes frightened her. His empty smile in no way warmed her. "Not soon enough."

Still stunned minutes later, Beth couldn't even hear through the noise of her blood rushing as they went back inside. The judge resumed his seat and began speaking. He mentioned foreseeing Hector having to answer some severe new accusations in the short future.

Beth heard the fateful words only barely, still struggled to swallow the sour dose of truth Landon had given her. *He couldn't wait to get rid of her.*

"Custody awarded to the petitioners…effective immediately…"

The verdict gradually sunk into her thoughts. She saw the judge rise to leave and Hector's stunned re-action. She noticed Landon shaking Mason's hand. Beth blinked, swayed as she rose to her feet.

Had they won?

So fast? She'd waited months and had expected her misery to last days and days, and now they'd *won?*

The rest happened in a flurry of movement. Being hugged by the Gages, by her mother, her father, by everyone but Landon.

Outside, after a wait that felt eternal, Beth squinted as she watched a car pull over, and David stepped out, running toward her with a grin and another drawing. She glanced at Anna, who smiled at them both from the bottom steps of the courthouse.

"Anna, thank you," she murmured under her breath, then quickly started for her son. God, was she *dreaming?* She wanted to sing and cry and dance.

"Mom! Mom, I made us a drawing!" He didn't kiss or hug her but immediately showed the paper to her and pointed at the figures drawn. "You, me and dog man. See!"

Beth's stomach clenched. The gigantic brown dog he'd drawn covered nearly half the page, and the rest of the picture contained David, Beth and Landon, holding hands while straddling the monster dog. "But sweetie, dog man…" *Won't be around for long.*

She fell quiet when Landon walked up beside her. "Dog man is taller in person," she improvised, flustered as she straightened. Her mom's sad, sympathetic look made a lump grow in her throat. Why was it when you made one dream come true, another fell apart?

Landon remained at her side, and all she became aware of was the fact that he didn't touch her. "Home?" he asked.

Temporary home, Beth thought, already pained to expose David to Landon's household. He couldn't get too settled in, could he?

Beth seized David's hand and tried a smile that didn't quite make it. "We're ready." God, that tiny hand inside of hers felt so right.

Ducking his head to meet David eye to eye,

Landon bumped fists with her son, both of them smiling and doing it naturally this time. "You can sleep in Nathan's room," he told the child.

The generous offer only made Beth's misery complete. For she, better than anyone, knew how zealously Landon had guarded that room. Before he'd known the truth about his baby.

Thomas opened the car door, and the three of them climbed inside, David excited, Landon quiet and Beth torn between excitement and despair, on their way to a make-believe home.

She and David hugged all the way.

Fourteen

The house was silent tonight.

Four months had passed, and every day of living with a fake family had been silent, wretched torture.

Landon stared out the window, not really seeing the manicured lawns outside. He was in his room, alone. Just him and the divorce papers. His bedroom had never felt so empty. The furniture couldn't fill the space. Nothing could fill the vast feeling of loss and emptiness.

Mask and Brindle, who'd taken to sleeping with David now, were down the hall in the boy's room.

And Beth…

He didn't know where she was. What she was doing. They barely spoke a word to each other. He knew she worked long hours at the computer during the day, and that she waited by the window when David arrived from school. He knew she slept with the door halfway open to hear anything amiss in David's room at night.

He knew that sometimes, when tired, she spoke in her dreams. And he knew that most of those times, she spoke his name. He'd also heard her cry once. Soft sniffles at midnight, coming from her room, making him toss in his empty bed wondering why she cried. He didn't hold his breath thinking it was him she cried for.

They'd been with him for four months now, four months and twenty nine days. Living with them felt like living with a ticking time bomb.

It was impossible to explain to Garrett, who'd been asking questions, or to anyone, what he'd been feeling all this time, seeing Beth every day, seeing her son frolicking out in the gardens during the afternoon. Her son, who was the same age Nathan would've been.

Longing didn't hold a candle to the emotions that bombarded him. Now his every muscle was taut with tension, tension which could find no relief, no kind of comfort. Because the tension that most gnawed at his gut stretched between Beth and him—and it was always home as long as she was.

He had to get rid of them, both of them.

He had known, from the moment he'd seen her in his hotel room, that she attracted him. He was a man accustomed to analyzing before acting, and he'd believed he'd somehow be able to remain immune to Beth's effect on him.

He hadn't.

Just as he hadn't predicted how badly he wanted to make things right for her. Even in ways he hadn't been able to make them right for himself.

No matter what she'd done to him, no matter that she'd lied and betrayed him, Landon had given her his word. She would have her son back at any cost, and Landon would have Halifax's head.

It had been four months and twenty nine days. Why had he not celebrated his victory over Halifax yet?

Because she's still here.

Landon wrenched off his tie, shoving it into his pants pocket. Halifax didn't deserve to be walking on the same planet Beth and her son were. And therefore, he would not. He was answering to a hell of a lot more charges now and would probably spend the rest of his life behind bars. Not only had the insurance companies sued him for millions the man in all likelihood did not have, but the District Attorney had charged him with distribution of illegal substances, and criminally negligent *manslaughter*. His situation was bleak.

As bleak as…Landon's bedroom.

"Damn it," he cursed. Before he knew what he did, he removed his coat, rolled the cuffs of his shirt, yanked the door open, and scoured the house for his wife.

She'd tried talking to him several times, always uneasily, but the intense sting of betrayal he felt kept building inside of him, and it left no room for listening to Beth. No room for coddling her. No room for anything except waiting to recover whatever life he'd had before her, and forget he'd ever married her.

He found the door to her bedroom partway open. Something tightened inside him as he pushed it wider and gazed into the dimly lit room. "Beth? Can we talk?"

Beth sat at the vanity, brushing her hair as though the act calmed her, and stopped when she heard him. She spun around on the upholstered ottoman with wide unblinking eyes, her mouth slightly parted. The picture of Halifax leaning in unbearably close to those pretty pink lips came back to Landon, making him want to rip down the drapes and toss them out the window.

He wanted to grab her shoulders and shake her,

take her, but instead his hands curled in on themselves, clenching tight at his sides.

"I thought you were at dinner with your brothers," Beth said.

"They were irritating me, so I left them to irritate each other." He propped a shoulder against the door frame, struggling to steady his heartbeat. He'd been inventing dinners all week—anything to stay away from home. From her. But tonight was different. "I merely wanted to see if you were all right."

Her smile held a hint of sadness. "So now you're talking to me."

He did not deny his lack of attention. How could he? He didn't want to see her, couldn't stand eating with her, could barely keep on living in the same house with her without going insane. Holding her little hand in his at court had been painful. Hearing her say she loved him with the same mouth she'd both kissed and lied to him had been among the most painfully mocking things in his entire goddamned life.

She rose to her feet in an easy, effortless move that made her body sway under the loose pastel green robe she wore. "Landon, about what I said at court—"

"I didn't come here to talk about what you said," he interrupted.

The hurt that came to her eyes made him want to charge across and do something to erase it. But she quickly wiped her expression clean, and he quickly dashed the thought of doing anything for her except what he'd promised he would and had already accomplished. Getting her son back.

Made visibly nervous by his visit, since he'd been doing a damned fine job of staying away from her room for weeks, Beth chewed her lower lip. "What did you come up here to talk about, then?"

I wanted to look at you one last time.

"I came to let you know…" His blood swirled. After the brutal feel of his own exposure at court, admitting to a room full of people what he had not admitted even to himself, every atom, cell and nerve in his body vibrated with yearning for her. Every night, every day. He had to leave, now, before he regretted it. He clamped his teeth and shook his head, frustrated with himself. "Forget it."

He spun around, but she called his name.

"Landon!"

He stiffened, and his head came up a bit, but he didn't turn until several slow, painful seconds passed. He faced her once more, not wanting to notice how her hair fell in a golden waterfall past her shoulders, framing her delicate face, not wanting to think that she looked vulnerable and beautiful and ready for bed.

"It's about the divorce, isn't it," she said.

Something cracked inside, but he'd be dead before he showed it. He nodded. "I wanted to say goodbye."

The next day started easily enough, ordinarily enough, except for the yellow folder Beth found on her nightstand. Landon must have gotten close to leave it there during the night, and her stomach tumbled realizing she must have slept through it.

So...

It was indeed goodbye.

During the morning she felt numb. Couldn't bring herself to open it. But she knew what it was. She accompanied Thomas to drop David at school, then she called her mother to let her know they'd be coming over today and staying for a week or two, until she could rent the small one-bedroom house at Crownridge she'd spotted.

David would miss the dogs. Between packing for them both and stealing sidelong glances at the envelope, Beth scoured through the dog books in Landon's study in search of the right breed for them. Maybe a little dog, which wouldn't bark and disturb the neighbors. She pored over the books, and stopped at: Old English Mastiffs.

Her insides wrenched as she read the description. *So.* This was why Landon didn't have a Doberman, or a German Shepherd. Mastiffs were loyal to the death. And it struck her how, above anything else, her husband valued loyalty, and how Beth had disappointed him.

She and David moved out that afternoon, before Landon returned from work, but even then, she didn't dare open the envelope.

She found herself staring at it the next morning, torn between finding out its contents or setting it on fire in the kitchen stove.

"Your father says Hector's going to get a life sentence, and there's really nothing he can do about it but serve it. Beth! Are you listening to me? I don't appreciate seeing you moping, Bethy. We really must do something about it."

Beth sat at the small old breakfast table—the envelope next to her plate. Outside, cars drove by. But no. No black Navigator or blue Maserati pulled over in front of Mom's home. Probably, there never would be.

She sipped her coffee, wondering what to do, wondering if she'd always been such a coward, when her mother's frequent, worried glances prodded her to speak. "I heard you," she said at last, sighing. "Hector's getting at least thirty years. I'm sorry,

Mother, but I'm not pretending to be surprised. The man had gotten away with it for too long."

"Speak louder, Bethy, I'm not wearing my hearing aid. And stop looking at those papers and open them, for heaven's sake. Here. Take this knife."

Okay, then.

Opening them now.

Beth's hand trembled as she sliced into the top folded edge, her pulse jumping in fear. "We agreed on this, you know," she said, to the kitchen in general. But had they agreed on kissing each other senseless? On telling each other secrets, fears, opening themselves up for heartbreak?

The memory of Landon telling her—*Before you give me anything else, Beth, I want your trust*—made her eyes start to burn. He'd given her his own trust, clearly. And she'd proved it a mistake.

"Well? Are those divorce papers?"

"Yes." Beth clutched them to her chest as though they were a declaration of love, while in her mind she imagined ripping, stomping on or losing them. Landon thought this was it, then? That she'd just take the papers and not be allowed an explanation? Not allowed a formal goodbye other than that brief, angry visit he'd paid her room last night? "Mom, can I borrow Dad's car for a bit?" Beth said, loudly enough for her mother to hear.

"Oh yes yes, of course!"

She fell deep into thought as she drove, the envelope her only passenger.

Now with her business up and running, she could find a place—nearby, in the same school district. And buy a car. She could start over as she'd always wanted to. Her and David, against the world.

But not before she saw Landon.

Dread coiled around her throat as she was led into his office. Then, coming around the desk in all his glory was Landon Gage. His was a face she would not see every day again, a voice she would not hear again. Here was a man who wanted to get rid of her.

On tenterhooks, Beth lowered herself on to the chair across the desk from his. "I thought I'd personally bring you these," she said, then cleared her throat and slightly raised the envelope to his attention.

"Not necessary." His timbre was about as inanimate as a lamp.

Beth bit her lip, then, trembling, set the papers on his desk. "I also thought you'd want this back." The small diamond on her finger flashed as she twisted off the ring.

She laid it over the envelope with a tiny but deafening "click".

Neither could bear to look at it.

Landon reclined in his seat and clasped his hands behind his head, his eyes slowly raking her body. "How are you? How's David?"

She smiled, tremulously, and wondered how she could even manage it. *Just as you managed to sign the divorce papers, Beth.* Very grudgingly.

"Happy. David's happy. Landon…thank you. You did as you promised and you were so good to me." So good for me…

She counted the prizes hanging behind his wall, recognitions of him as a newspaper genius, and tried to calm down. Once, when she was little, she'd shattered her tiniest, most prized crystal figurine into what seemed like a hundred little pieces. It was a swan her mother had given her, and she had treasured it. But no matter how much she prayed, the figurine was beyond repair, the shards so tiny they only cut and cut at her fingers when she tried to mend it. Was that the case with Landon? She could wish and pray and want but she would only cut herself more. He didn't look at her with warmth. He looked at her not like a husband, but an enemy. They. *They* were beyond repair. But she had to try.

"If that's all…" He shuffled some papers—and Beth got the message clearly, even though he spoke again in interest. "Kate tells me you're officially a partner in her business."

She waited for him to say more, something about them, words welling in her throat. No. She should not do this. She would divorce him and she would bury her past and start a new life for herself. But she did not want a divorce. She wanted, needed forgiveness. Her own and his. And love. It still thickened her veins, danced in her thoughts and in her heart. Her nerves quivered. Inside, she screamed. *Love me back. Have pity on me and hold me...like before... like when you loved me with your body....*

"Business, yes. We're doing great with online advertising on our recipe section."

"Good. Very good, Bethany."

"Landon, why are we doing this?" she blurted. "Why won't you listen to me?"

One eyebrow lifted, as though he could not for the life of him have heard correctly. "We had an agreement. We've fulfilled both our ends."

"So what happened between us...? We're to pretend it never happened at all?"

"Beth," he said with a significant pause, and she could see him grapple for words. "I expect...things of my wife."

He left them unsaid, the things he wanted.

His voice dropped a decibel, became a terse, quiet

confession. "Is it wrong that I expect you to be loyal and truthful with me?"

Beth gulped as she watched him rise, eager to dismiss her. She leapt to her feet. "What if I was trying to protect you? What if you have me all wrong? I'm not who you think I am, Landon! If you'd only let me show you…"

He went rigid when she sailed around the desk.

"Bethany—" He caught her shoulders, but didn't push her away. "We were a bad idea. I thought I could live with it, knowing you were Halifax's first, but I can't. I can't stand the idea. I can't stand the idea of you…lying to me."

"I can't stand it either, but I can't change the past, please understand. I just didn't want to *hurt* you."

Frantically, she slid her palm up his shirt, his chest solid, hot through the cotton. She could feel every sinew of muscle underneath. Deep, forgotten places inside her clenched. "Landon, please."

"Beth, what are you playing at?" His voice grew husky. Desire trembled there. His hand on her back began to squeeze her, began to want and feel and knead.

She pressed closer, a little in agony, seeking ease for the horrible burn growing inside her. "Last night

I saw you… I thought my husband came to get his good-night kiss."

He groaned. Images of his sculpted body began to tease and tantalize her. Him in nakedness, the male form in all its glory, chiseled like a statue but warmer. Just one time—they'd been together just one time—and it haunted her. She pressed her legs together and tried to breathe slowly. But the images remained. Clearer, more vivid. They were memories. Of when he'd been inside her. Of him biting at her breasts. Of her nails sinking into his back. Of that consuming passion they had shared.

He pressed her back against the window, caging her in with his body. "Damn you."

He swept down—but stopped a hairbreadth away. Opening her mouth, she flicked her tongue out to lick the firm flesh of his lips. Explosions of colors. Mouths melding. Skin, heat, ecstasy. "Is this wrong?" she taunted. She draped a leg around his thigh and flattened herself against his chest, her breasts crushed against his ribs, her tummy to his. "How can this be wrong?"

"I don't…" His hand fisted in her hair and he opened his mouth, giving her the mist of his breath. She waited for that kiss, the searing kiss that would put everything behind them. It didn't come. "Want you anymore," he huskily murmured, the graze of his lips across hers so bare and fleeting she mewled with a protest for more.

His hold tightened on her hair before he released her. "Goodbye, Miss Lewis."

Fifteen

Landon prowled the city, simmering with pent-up need, anger and despair. He couldn't bear to go home. It felt empty, the house, his room, his bed. Beth was gone, and the relief he'd assumed he'd feel with her departure wasn't coming.

He couldn't stop thinking about her, what she'd said about a ten-month-old baby. How she'd looked in his office, desperate as that first day, this time desperate for something Landon could no longer give her.

He drove along the highway, and before he knew where he headed, Landon stopped by Mission Park cemetery. His son's gravestone; he'd visited only once before years ago. Why now? Why was he back here at this place that held his most haunting memories?

Because he's my son.

He gazed down at the lettering, engraved in the granite headstone. Nathaniel Gage.

He's not your son, he's Hector's...

To hear his own wife say it had been a blow, but once the words registered, he'd felt more than anger, more than despair. He'd felt betrayed and played and violated.

They'd won at court—but the satisfaction of winning hadn't accompanied the success. Landon had lost. Because it was just the kind of cruel twist of fate that Landon should love something of his enemy's. It was just the kind of cruel twist of fate that even knowing Nathan was not his son, and belonged to the bastard, Landon still loved him.

Nathaniel was a Gage.

He stroked a hand over the curved top of the gravestone. He didn't understand. He never would. One second his attention was elsewhere, and when he'd looked back his wife and kid were gone. The accident had revealed her treachery. Phone calls, emails, letters. Years betraying him behind his back. But never had he imagined it had dated to before. Before Landon had met her, before he'd married her.

To think how she'd snagged him, young and in his prime, pretending he was the father of her unborn child. For the length of their short marriage Landon had been faithful, making an effort, for her, for Nathaniel. And all that time, she'd been seeing Hector.

His son would've been thirsty for life.

And Chrystine's treachery robbed him of it.

But now, even now, when he'd taken everything of Halifax's, his practice, his respect and his freedom, Landon could not enjoy the victory. He could not go back to the way he was before. He loved that son, wanted him as his, and the path of revenge had opened up a whole new wanting for him.

He wanted Bethany—the son she and Halifax had. That, too, he wanted. Because it was hers.

Yes, a cruel twist of fate it was. To love the two things that had first belonged to the enemy.

A bouquet of flowers appeared out of nowhere— white roses suddenly laid there, over the grave, tied by a sleek white ribbon. Landon glanced past his shoulder to confirm his suspicions, and sighed.

He wasn't alone. Comfortably clad in a flowery dress and a pair of maroon cowboy boots, his mother nailed the Texan matron look down to a tee.

"What are you doing here?"

"I come here every week. Why wouldn't I visit my grandson?" Her weathered hand stroked the name, and Landon lowered his face, said softly, "He's not mine, Mother."

She didn't jerk at the news, only regarded him with that impenetrable coolness of hers. "You were always the one ready to make the tough decisions for the family. And I think you're so used to making them, you can't believe anything can be good and simple anymore."

"Nothing in my life has ever been good or simple."

"But it is. Bethany fell in love with you. And you with her. Good. And simple."

Landon didn't respond, fought not to think of her, remember the ways her lips curled into all kinds of mischievous or shy or soft smiles.

He tossed a twig into the air. "I'm not sure she loves me. I'm not even sure what was real and what wasn't."

"I know what you were fighting for, Landon. You've never been vindictive. You've always done the honorable thing. You weren't fighting for revenge, you were fighting for a family. The family you deserve. A woman touched your heart, even when you didn't want her to, and you were fighting for her. Are you going to quit now? When you're so far ahead in the game?"

He remembered her. Her dense lashes had glittered with tears. She'd annihilated his mind and senses. How could she have filtered through his defenses?

Because he'd seen her uniqueness and he'd let her.

And she'd let him in, as well.

And he knew then that he would have no other family.

But the one he'd already claimed before the world as his.

Exactly one month after moving in with her parents, Beth wiped a hand across her moistened brow and sighed in satisfaction as she gazed across her new one-bedroom home. Only five closed boxes remained, stacked neatly to one side of the small foyer, but compared to the forty loaded monsters she'd started with, what remained was nothing.

Easily tackled in an hour, if not less.

Sighing, she opened the front door to check if any boxes remained out on the porch and frowned when she spotted a small one.

The plain brown box sat meekly on her doorstep, just over the new rug that read "Welcome."

Beth didn't remember having seen it there before.

Confusion mingled with curiosity as she shook the box. Something thudded inside. "What the…" Her hands flew to open the package.

A brand-new little black book. That's exactly what she discovered.

A brand-spanking-new little black book exactly like the one that had once brought her and Landon together. Halifax was in jail and wouldn't ever bother her or David. So why this sense of nervousness at the sight of the new book? And where, God, where, did this strange excitement come from?

Because it reminds you of the day you met Landon...

Her throat filled up with emotion at the bittersweet memory, and, carefully, afraid of what she'd find, or maybe more afraid of what she wouldn't find, Beth opened the book to page one.

Her pulse shot up. There, inside, on the first page, lay a note, written in Landon's handwriting. She read the note once, failing to go back for a second read when her eyes blurred. It was a silly note, from a man who'd always criticized anyone for writing his sins in a little black book. And now he was writing one of his.

Landon Gage is a fool, it read.

Eyes stinging, Beth looked up and saw him as a big dark blur. Him. He was there, standing there, his presence warm as a sun. He stood on the steps of her new home, looking clean and manly and slightly rumpled without a tie.

Beth blinked, feeling like a thousand angels were sweeping her off her feet, but it was only one man. Just one man, a prince to her.

A frisson of expectation went through her as she waited for him to say something, *please* say something, because she seemed to have lost the ability to speak.

He leaned against the front porch balustrade, under the shade, watching her somberly. "Hi."

Stifling a tremor that rushed from the top of her head down to the tips of her toes, Beth clutched the book to her body, still unable to believe he stood here, in the flesh, at her doorstep. "Hi, Landon."

God, she'd missed the sight of Landon Gage. She felt it proper to say something, but her mouth felt like a prison for all the words she wanted to say and couldn't.

She drank up his image as if she were seeing him for the very first time, examining the fit of his clean tailored slacks and button-down shirt, remembering the lean, hard body underneath. He'd cut his hair, and he looked very young and very handsome.

With a halfhearted smile, Landon took a step closer. "There's this man I need you to exact revenge upon. An imbecile who was about to make the biggest mistake of his life," he said direly.

His voice did things to her, awakened her body so

that her senses swam. Flutters invaded her, whizzing in her chest, her stomach, her head. "So that's what the book is for," she said.

"It's for revenge, Bethany." Landon's forehead creased as he took yet another step closer. "He's undeserving, this man. Extremely undeserving. And I can think of no one else who could torture him as well as you."

"Torture him?" Her temperature jacked up another degree.

He gave a slight nod. "Uh-huh. I need you to stare him in the face, every day, so he remembers what he almost let another man take away from him. I need you to be ruthless, to have absolutely no mercy on him, and above all, I want you to make him pay. It's a matter of revenge, Beth. And this man…" The determination in his eyes arrested her. "This man is begging for it."

She didn't laugh. She could tell by the tension in him, in his face, that it cost him his pride and ego and everything he valued to say it.

Oh, God, Landon was begging for *her*.

Her palms itched to touch him but instead she wrapped her arms around herself, unsure of how to verbalize her sentiments. Sentiments in the lines of: *I love you, yes yes yes, amen to whatever you're proposing!*

Should she invite him inside? She wanted to. But the house was still a mess, and her pride smarted at the mere thought of Landon discovering that she'd be living with only the bare necessities. Then she realized that in a faded T-shirt, shorts and sandals, she wasn't much of an improvement over her small, plain home.

"Sounds like a good plan." She remained in place at the doorway, unsure of what to do next. Her heart pounded a mile a minute and she still struggled to catch her breath. "But there's one problem."

He went rigid. He surveyed the empty lots that flanked her house, where in the future she'd have neighbors. "A problem," he said. His jaw squared, and when the wind blew in her direction, it brought his clean scent of soap with it.

She hauled in a good lungful of him, unable to stop a shudder. "A big problem." She stepped out into the porch. Closer to him.

His eyebrows slanted over his eyes, and wearing that worried frown, Landon Gage looked adorable. He pinched the bridge of his nose as though trying to stifle a headache. "What kind of problem?"

Beth could barely speak, the emotions rising inside her too powerful to rein back. "That I have no more hate left."

She canted her face to his, and the feelings of

passion and need she felt for him overflowed her. Heat spread across her midsection while a swirl of desire took form in his glinting silver eyes.

"I have only one feeling lately, apart from sadness, and I have so much of it I don't know what to do with it."

The features of his face went taut with emotion as he took one more step, the final step. The one that brought him so close she could feel his breath, his heat, inhale his scent. "What is it that you feel, Beth?" He stood only inches from her, tall and dark and patient and so male she felt coy and shy.

She wanted to touch him, wanted to so much, but for the moment lacked the courage. "Like I said, I don't know what to do with it."

It was Landon who couldn't seem to help himself any longer. Pain streaked through his face, tightening his features as he moved. He framed her cheeks with his hands, his fingertips caressing her temples. "I love you, Mrs. Gage." His chest expanded under his shirt as he inhaled and set his forehead on hers. "I love you and I want you to tell me you feel this for me, that you love me, only me."

Her body responded to his evocative words, to his calling her by his name. Her blood bubbled in her veins. A head-tingling sensation swept through her and it made her faint.

He wanted her; he was here for her. And Beth wasn't going to make him beg.

Never, not for a moment in the past months, had she been confused about this. Him. And the fact that she wanted to be with him. She'd dreamt every night over the past lonely weeks, waiting, praying, that Landon would come to terms with the specialness of what they had together. That he'd love her more than her pride and realize Beth was not Chrystine.

Beth loved him. Had been spoiled for any other man but Landon.

She'd settle for nothing less than him.

"I meant what I said in court, Landon." She took his jaw in her hands, her eyelids fluttering as she rose on tiptoe to brush his lips with hers. *"I love you."*

Her soft kiss seemed to take him by surprise, and it took him a moment to take action, but then he released a low, rough groan. He encircled her waist and kissed the breath out of her, his hands wandering her curves, gripping her tight against him.

He exhaled as though he'd been holding his breath for too long. "God, Bethany." He leaned in again, this time taking her mouth slowly and deeply, savoring her taste, allowing her to savor his, then he took her hands between both of his. "I'm sorry," he murmured huskily against her. "I'm sorry for being such a fool."

"I'm sorry for not telling you about Nathan."

"I'm sorry you ever married that bastard, Beth, and that I almost let him take you away from me."

"And I'm sorry I ever met him! But then, maybe…" A thought struck her, and it was so funny, she smiled. "But then he brought us together, didn't he, Landon?"

Amusement lightened his expression, and a fingertip came up to still her lips. "The only good thing he did in his sorry-ass life. Beth, I need you. I need my wife. Marry me again. For real this time. No hidden agendas. Just two people who want to spend the rest of their lives together."

Beth grabbed his shoulders and kissed him, kissed him hard and felt him respond to her with fierce hunger, and her breath shortened until she panted. "Our first marriage was realer than anything in my life. I didn't want to get divorced."

Out of his back pockets, Landon yanked out a roll of papers and without ceremony tore them up, scattering the snow-like pieces across the porch. "Then we won't."

"Were those the—"

"Divorce papers? They were before I ripped

them." He signaled toward the house, his eyes alight with mischief. "Want some help moving out?"

"Oh, God, I just moved in."

"Show me around then?"

She laughed. "I know what you want, Mr. Gage." She gestured him into the house and kissed him again. "The mattress will arrive later," she murmured seductively.

He kicked the door shut and imprisoned her against him, her breasts crushed against his chest, her buttocks in his big massaging hands. "We don't need a mattress." He spoke huskily against her. "All we need to start again is this." He pulled out another roll of papers from behind him. "I'm sure you'll enjoy burning this prenup. We'll have another one drawn."

"So we can discuss intimacy with your lawyers? No, thank you!"

"So we can discuss my millions and millions and how much you want."

Frowning, Beth seized the prenup and ripped it in two, because trust begot trust, and she wanted to start with lots of it. "I just want you, because you're you, and not for any other reason."

He broke into a smile and squeezed her hard. "Damn, Beth, that's about the sexiest thing I've ever heard."

"Wait until I tell you about the little red number I was wearing at court."

He swept down and seized her lips with his, and he kissed her with hunger and heat, stroked the sides of her body while he raked his teeth down her neck, over her shoulder, pulled her faded T-shirt down to reveal her flesh and swirl his tongue against her collarbone. "I don't care about the red number. I care about what's beneath it. About this. My wife, and how fast I can get you naked."

Clinging to him, she kissed him for all the times she hadn't kissed him. "I'm all yours, Gage."

* * * * *

Mills & Boon® Online

Discover more romance at
www.millsandboon.co.uk

 FREE online reads

 Books up to one
month before shops

 Browse our books
before you buy

...and much more!

For exclusive competitions and instant updates:

 Like us on **facebook.com/romancehq**

 Follow us on **twitter.com/millsandboonuk**

 Join us on **community.millsandboon.co.uk**

Visit us Online Sign up for our FREE eNewsletter at
www.millsandboon.co.uk